PENGUIN BOOKS

OTHER PEOPLE'S CHILDREN

Lydia Gerend was born in Wisconsin in 1943. In 1965 she moved to England and lived in Exeter, Cambridge, Whitby, Leeds and Lancaster before settling on a Yorkshire hill farm. She trained and worked as a librarian, but in 1977 left work to write full time. She has also completed a large three-part novel, *Dark Singer*, which explores some of the mythological and psychological aspects of the mother image.

LYDIA GEREND

Other People's Children

A NOVEL

PENGUIN BOOKS

FOR NUBBY AND GERT

Penguin Books Ltd, 27 Wrights Lane, London w8 5tz (Publishing and Editorial)
and Harmondsworth, Middlesex, England (Distribution and Warehouse)
Viking Penguin Inc., 40 West 23rd Street, New York, New York 10010, USA
Penguin Books Australia Ltd, Ringwood, Victoria, Australia
Penguin Books Canada Ltd, 2801 John Street, Markham, Ontario, Canada l3r 1b4
Penguin Books (NZ) Ltd, 182–190 Wairau Road, Auckland 10, New Zealand

First published by Viking 1986
Published in Penguin Books 1987

Copyright © Lydia Gerend, 1986
All rights reserved

Made and printed in Great Britain by
Hazell Watson & Viney Limited,
Member of the BPCC Group,
Aylesbury, Bucks
Filmset in Monophoto Ehrhardt

1

I was four years old when I decided never to have children. My sister Camille was two at the time, and though she witnessed the same event, on her it had the opposite effect.

'Pretty,' she cooed, on seeing Mrs Potter's newborn baby asleep at last in its mother's sweaty arms.

I stared at Camille, disbelieving. How—?

It was the winter of 1946/7, later called the worst of the century. Not to us it wasn't. Daddy, nostalgic for his Michigan childhood, had bought us skates for Christmas. We hadn't started school yet and so spent most of our time on the small pond which marked both the edge of our garden and the end of our London suburb. With the bigger bullies trapped in school, we had it almost to ourselves. Bliss. Like flying, it was, even after just a couple of months' practice.

We were setting off for the pond when Mrs Potter went into labour. We heard her through the partition wall. If our semi had had thicker walls we still would have heard her. I think every house on the street must have heard her.

Mummy stopped plucking dead blooms from the pot of forced freesias on the sideboard and frowned. The window was a jungle of frost-ferns which hissed if you ran a fingernail across them, but that isn't what Mummy was frowning at. She was frowning at the street beyond, glassy with ice the gritters never got to till the day was nearly over. Ice equals no midwife equals… She dropped the squashed flowers on the sideboard.

'Put your coats on,' she said, though we already had. Then she put on her own and pushed us out of the house. I was delighted – I thought she was coming to the pond with us. Instead, she pushed us through Mrs Potter's doorway.

If Mummy had let us go skating she might have had more grandchildren today.

The house was even colder than ours. The baby – Mrs Potter's first – wasn't due for another week and Mr Potter had gone off to work leaving his wife to light the fires. Her mother was supposed to be coming from Birmingham in a few days to help out.

'Phone the midwife,' Mrs Potter groaned. The last syllable crescendoed to wwaaAAAAIIII and never finished. Mummy fled down the stairs to the phone. We fled up the stairs. Naturally we wanted to be where the action was. We peered in.

An enormous blue balloon occupied most of the bed. Above it, severed by the blanket's edge, was a crumpled red face and a scrap of soggy hair. The mouth was open in a tight O which seemed to draw all the lines of the face into it and feed the terrible sound. This was not the baby; it was Mrs Potter.

Behind us, Mummy's voice was rising up the stairs. 'That's two miles away!' she told the telephone. 'I need someone *now*!'

In front of us Mrs Potter's voice was also rising. 'I'LL KILL THE BLOODY BASTARD!'

The receiver went down with a ping. Mummy's coat swished up the stairs. She was composing her face in a cheerful smile. 'The midwife will be just a tiny bit delayed,' she sang out. 'She has to walk, you know.'

'HE CAN BLOODY WELL HAVE THE NEXT ONE HIMSELF!'

Mummy's smile vanished. She grabbed our coat collars and pushed us away from the door.

Why didn't she let us go skating?

The midwife never came – we later learned that she slipped on the ice and sprained her ankle. It didn't matter. Mummy had switched into emergency gear. She lit the fires, heated the water, fetched towels and scissors and string and I don't know what else. I don't know either how long we stood there. We had drifted back to the door, only this time we had the sense to press ourselves against the wall every time Mummy swished past. She didn't even see us.

Neither did Mrs Potter, heaving and jerking and screaming all over the bed. At some stage the blankets disappeared and the balloon became flesh-coloured. And then, after a terrific yell which rattled the windows (maybe it was the wind), there appeared between Mrs Potter's swollen legs a glistening mound of blood-drenched meat. I turned away and put my hands to my mouth. I had once seen a run-over dog and was trying not to be sick.

Camille hadn't seen the dog. She was watching everything, fascinated.

It was a long time before I dared to look again. When I did, Mummy was holding something up by what looked like legs and nervously tapping it. Clearly she expected something to happen. She tapped again, harder. Still no action. She gave it an angry shake and finally it emitted a faint wheeze. Blood was still dripping from it. Mummy was swaying slightly. Her eyes looked crossed. I turned away again.

'It's a boy,' said Mummy's voice.

There was no response.

'Don't you want to see your son?' said Mummy softly.

Silence.

I risked a quick look.

The baby had been placed on Mrs Potter's chest. Mrs Potter had her head turned away from it. I wondered if she'd seen the dead dog, too. Her eyes were closed.

'Pretty,' cooed Camille.

I stared at her, disbelieving. How— ?

Mummy shut the door.

A week later Mrs Potter brought the baby over for us to see. It didn't look like much but at least the blood was gone. Mrs Potter looked like herself again: a merry little brunette like Mummy. She couldn't praise Mummy enough, said she was just as much a hero as Daddy. Daddy laughed. 'That's for sure,' he said. 'I'd rather fly through a hundred enemy aircraft than deliver a baby!' Everybody laughed. Mrs Potter thrust the baby at me. I shrank away. Everybody laughed again. She thrust it at Camille instead. Camille took it and beamed down at the limp face. Everybody said 'Aw' like they do in the cinema. Two years later Mrs Potter had another baby.

2

The reference to Daddy as 'hero' is a little misleading. At the beginning of the war he was in civil aviation. By the end of the war, as an officer in the USAF, he'd moved up and out into administration. The heroic bit came in the middle, when they were short of pilots and Daddy had to parachute supplies behind enemy lines. On the way back his plane was hit several times. The whole crew worked like hell to repair the damage and somehow got back in one piece. This was called heroic. Daddy called it 'saving our skins'. He never had any illusions about it.

By this time he was married to Mummy – they met on his first trip over. They married, mated and produced me, all within a year. Love at first sight, Mummy told us. There was a lot of it about in those days. I suppose the attraction was obvious. Here are their portraits, *c.* 1942:

Daddy. Tall dark and handsome. Quite a bit older than Mummy. Gallant towards women, loyal to his men, generous to everyone. A big smile, lots of laughter, and that unthinking self-confidence which is peculiar to Americans and even now passes for wisdom. People felt safe around Daddy. As long as the world was in his hands, everything would be okay. For women he provided the rare combination of excitement and security. Who could resist? Certainly not Mummy.

Mummy. Small dark and pretty with the famous English complexion and manners which, to my midwestern father,

9

must have seemed exquisite though they were standard to every middle-class English person then as now. Flowers were her hallmark: in the house, in her hair, on the feminine little dresses she managed to run up from the most unlikely of wartime materials. She could quote Wordsworth on daffodils, Burns on roses, Keats on lilies. She played 'Come Into the Garden, Maud' on the piano for him. She sang 'My Blue Heaven' for him. She made pumpkin pie out of marrows for him.

We lived with Mummy's parents during the war, Daddy visiting whenever he got leave. After the war he left the air force and joined Grandad's firm. Daddy was a genius with machines – planes, printing presses, it was all the same to him. He was also a genius with people (Americans were popular then) and soon moved up and out into administration again. By the time we moved to the house outside London, the farmer's boy from Michigan was as middle-class as Mummy.

3

My name is Holly and I was born on Christmas Day 1942. My sister followed some two years later. Being an autumn baby she was nearly called Daisy (Michaelmas), but my father thought that was going too far and brought my mother a bunch of camellias and that was that. God knows where he found them, what with the war and all.

I don't remember much about the war, or about my grandparents' house, or about my grandparents who were all dead by 1950. This is probably repression and if so works very well. I sometimes wonder about those years and all the missing traumas which might account for my not having children. The first I do remember is Mrs Potter; but by four, Freud says, we're already fixed. I wonder too why the same event affected Camille so differently. Assuming it affected either of us at all.

Ours was a standard yellow brick semi with a not-so-standard huge garden that was my mother's delight. Though she continued to dig for victory long after the war was over, it was the flowers she loved most. She hadn't been to university but somehow got to know of the Bloomsbury set and modelled her modest patch on Sissinghurst. Camille and I spent much of our early years in that garden (childhood summers are always sunny) and thought primary school a poor substitute. None the less, we did fairly well.

In novels, the narrator is usually the plain awkward bookish girl with glasses and no grace, while her frivolous sister is a pretty blonde who has lots of friends and is always laughing. This was not quite the case with us. It's true that Camille is small like our mother and I am large like our father (statuesque is the polite term). But we are both brown-haired, brown-eyed, and well matched in beauty and wit: not much of the former, a decent amount of the latter. We weren't even serious rivals; Camille was her mother's child, I was my father's. (I always feel sorry for third children. Who's left?) Apart from the usual thumpings and whining and hair-pulling and sulking, we got on well together. In fact, we actually liked each other's company – and for the most part, liked it better than that of other children.

I suppose I'm repressing again. Probably we hated each other. My childhood seems to smooth itself out into a pleasant past. Just that: pleasant. I suspect most people have children either to compensate for a rotten childhood or to relive an idyllic one. What do you do with a pleasant past? My main memory is of mild impatience. Adults said, 'Enjoy yourself while you can – it's the best time of your life.' I knew they were lying. Adulthood was clearly more desirable than childhood – otherwise why bother to grow up?

4

For a long time now I've lived in a market town in Yorkshire which my next-door neighbours describe as a Sloane Ranger playground. With shops full of cashmere sweaters and horse blankets and prissy china, I see what they mean. None the less, the play is pretty serious. Three large country estates converge on the town like giant slices of pie and influence every aspect of life, including the library, where I work. When Camille first joined CND she persuaded me to put some leaflets on the table near the door. This table normally displays the latest acquisitions (biographies, books on the Royal Family) and information on current events (a garden open day for Save the Children, local history talks, the church fête). I knew the leaflets were subversive and was glad. God, the joy of being able to *do* something! The raised eyebrows, the gentle frowns, the playful glance of approbation – all of this I met with my sweetest librarian's face. (Librarians are highly respected in such communities.) Then one day the leaflets disappeared. I was prepared for this. Camille had given me a large stock which I'd hidden in my office. Out they came, and from then on I manned the desk myself as much as possible to keep a watchful eye. Finally the mayor took me aside. He was very nice about it and so was I. I pointed to the rubber-stamped address at the bottom: it was the local branch of CND. Local, you see? They could do nothing, without offending democratic principles, till some years later a local branch of Women For Peace Through Defence started up and Mrs Trevelyan slapped a heap of rival leaflets down beside Camille's. What could I do? I too am bound by this democracy thing. Camille and I had a row over it.

She followed me everywhere: to school (the local grammar), to university (a northern redbrick) and finally to my Yorkshire market town. I didn't see anything sinister in it, and to this day I don't think she planned what she did to me.

The town has a broad main street which broadens further into a square complete with WW1 monument, town hall, library and some of the nicer shops. It's a nice street altogether, picturesque and loved by tourists. The council houses are nicely hidden and the little crime we have (underage drinking, drinking and driving, the odd vandalized phone box) is dealt with nicely by friendly old-fashioned policemen who sing in the choir and pat babies on the head. 'Ambridge lives,' says my boyfriend Barnaby, though our town is much bigger than Ambridge.

I live on the outskirts (as in London) in a small house with a big garden (as in London – I'm aware of these patterns). It's part of a terrace built for estate labourers and was, when I moved here seventeen years ago, occupied mainly by old people. The reason for this is simple. The front doors have only a narrow pavement separating them from a busy main road, while the houses themselves are tiny two-up-and-two-downs unsuitable for families. The terrace was derelict and downmarket, a gift for the young marrieds and singles who have since taken it over. I was young married, too, and I'd like to describe it as it was then, about a year after Andrew and I bought it, when we'd just got it looking nice.

It's on the left-hand side of the road as you come north into town and is the first one of the terrace. The squire intended building two more but never got around to it, so one of my predecessors bought up the two building plots and added them to the garden.

As you go in the front door, the stripped pine stairs are straight ahead, along the right-hand wall. On the left wall is a fireplace with a back boiler that heats the water and radiators. The living room is (was) small but cosy, with comfortable hand-me-down furniture and the Habitat type shelving popular at that time. There was a beautiful oriental rug on the floor – my aunt Beattie's wedding present to us – and a grandfather clock in one corner. There was a small Queen Anne style desk I bought with my first pay cheques. There was a stereo and all our records (mine were the Beethoven). There was a whole shelf full of the alabaster jars I used to collect. There were houseplants everywhere. There were a lot of things that aren't there any more.

The kitchen is long and narrow, irritatingly split in two by the back door. I cook on the left, eat on the right.

Upstairs, a double bedroom corresponds to the living room. There's a tiny bathroom in the middle, a tiny box-room at the back, and a lot of stairwell and corridor.

Most marriages have one room which becomes the battle-ground for different ideologies. Ours was the boxroom. Andrew said he needed a study (he was a teacher). I said we needed a guest room, guests should have a proper room and not have to sleep in the middle of a thoroughfare like our living room. The compromise was, like most marriages, an uneasy one. Andrew had his study, but when visitors came, we lugged his desk into our bedroom and tripped over it for the duration. Two big chunks of foam normally stored under our bed made a wall-to-wall double mattress between bookshelves. But one thing we did agree on: the boxroom was *not* to become a nursery.

5

I met Andrew on the Aldermaston march. This was in the mid-sixties, during my two years of flat-sharing in London. I'd graduated the year before and in September begun a course in librarianship, one of the two obvious careers open to those BA Hons. English who weren't plugged into the media. I needed a career because I was sure I'd never marry. It's not that I didn't want to. I just hadn't met anyone on whom I could try out the word 'husband' without laughing.

And then there was this large red and black lumberjack jacket in front of me. The hair above it was the regulation-long of the period (i.e. not very), blond, well-cut, clean. His jeans were clean, too. I was sure he was American, especially as he was carrying one of the YANKS OUT OF VIET-NAM placards. Beside him walked a matching Brünhilde. Simultaneously I (a) squashed a pang of disappointment, and (b) looked for the rings which, even if missing, would tell me nothing.

'A face like a bulldozer,' I speculated to Camille, compensating already.

So, there it is. I fell in love with the back of a lumberjack jacket. I didn't even wait for its wearer to turn around, which he did, a few minutes later, to reveal a fleshy but handsome face with wide-awake blue eyes scanning the crowd behind.

'Counting his followers,' whispered Camille.

I laughed – we shared a distrust of handsome faces – then

stopped. The blue eyes were on me. The face broadened into such an open smile that I felt ashamed of my thoughts and terrified of Camille's possibly overheard remark. To cancel both I flashed back a comradely smile of the sort appropriate to Aldermaston. He hesitated, as if contemplating speech, then nodded and turned away, leaving me with an odd sense of danger averted.

We didn't speak till Hyde Park, when I offered Brünhilde a brownie. It wasn't the innocent gesture it seemed. If American, she would show nostalgia; if English, curiosity. Either way, a reaction, an opening. By now I was just plain nosy.

'???' said Brünhilde.

'A brownie,' I explained. 'American.'

'Oh!' She glanced at Siegfried's placard resting on the grass. 'I hope you don't mind.'

'Of course not. Even my father agrees, and he used to be in the American air force. Hence,' I continued idiotically, 'the brownies. My mother,' the idiot concluded, 'had to learn to make them.'

Siegfried came to my rescue. 'Really? Why?'

I knew he didn't mean the brownies. 'You can't win a war if the enemy is militarily a great deal inferior to yourself.'

'I don't follow.'

'Ask Camille – she's studying politics,' I heard my voice say. Then I saw my body stretch out on the grass, leaving Camille to take over. It was an astonishing thing for me to do, totally out of character. Me, forever anxious, accommodating, eager to please. I rationalized: their accents (Essex) had satisfied my curiosity and I was tired, what with the long walk and too much food. Also, I'd been to a party the night before.

No, that wasn't it. The truth is, my interest in this stranger had concentrated itself into such an intense knot that I had to break it, and the best way was to deny it.

It was cold down there, but safe. You can't put a foot in a closed mouth. Above me the voices danced: Camille's earnest soprano, Brünhilde's smooth alto, a rumbling bass from Siegfried. Just like Daddy's, I thought. Big body, big voice, the same reassuring manner. *The world is safe in my hands.* I'd fallen for it again. I knew I was being rude, overcompensating for my annoyance at having wanted to impress these strangers and – worse – failed. What did it matter? I thought about *Tonio Kröger* and the mindless way the dark always envies the light, the south the north, the small the large (though who was I to talk?). They'd been brother and sister. And sure enough, above me Siegfried metamorphosed into Andrew and Brünhilde his twin sister Gillian. The blond beast lives. I hated them both. I grunted contemptuously and dozed off.

'Holly?'

The voice was intimate and amused. I looked up to see two large hands stretched out ready to pull me up from the grass. Without thinking, I took them.

What had happened in my absence? We moved back into the march a foursome. We walked in step. When the singing started, we sang in harmony. Our cheers in Trafalgar Square rose as one, and when we finally dispersed, I wasn't at all surprised that Andrew asked for my phone number.

On the other hand, I wasn't surprised when he didn't use it. A silent fortnight later I concluded: march mania, ideological euphoria. (The Aldermaston was like that in those days.)

And then the phone rang.

And a fortnight later, again.

A week's interval the next time.

Another week.

Five days.

Two.

A year later, in June 1966, we were married.

We chose a registry office. Mummy was heartbroken. She'd had an austerity wedding and now she was missing her second chance, too.

'But Andrew and I are atheists,' I said.

'You know that's not true.' Then she smiled her mystical smile. 'Deep down in your heart of hearts,' she said, 'you believe in Something, Someone. Everyone does.'

'I don't.'

Poor Mummy. Deep down in her heart of hearts, she didn't believe either. What she craved was the building, a pretty little stone and stained glass church left over from the village our suburb had been before London ate it up. We went at Christmas and Easter, Mummy always criticizing the flowers, saying how much better she would have done them, which was true.

The reception was nice, though. Mummy had her way there, and the house was so full of flowers there was hardly room for the people. And there were a lot of people. Neither of us had many relatives, but there were my flatmates, a few old schoolfriends and neighbours, friends from university, Andrew's colleagues from the public school where he taught Latin, his Cambridge cronies, etcetera. The life and soul, though, was my aunt. Usually aunts and uncles are the sludgy bit at a reception, but Beattie had presence. This had nothing to do with her appearance: tall, thin, no-nonsense, a spinsterish bluestocking who dressed severely when she took the trouble and sloppily when she didn't. There was nothing defiant about her clothes – she just kept forgetting to think about them. She was scarcely conscious of herself from the neck down. Only heads mattered, her own and other people's. Beattie could draw the intellect out of a cretin, which she certainly had to do with some of her students. It wasn't because of her I chose the northern redbrick where she taught, but had I, rather than Camille, had the flair for politics, I might have chosen that for the sake of her lectures. I picture her now at our reception and out of respect forget what she wore. All I see is an alert little head on its stalk, the bright beady eyes missing nothing. Her laugh is just short of raucous as she baits one of Andrew's cousins, a minor gentleman farmer, in a friendly little chat about agriculture in which he is startled to discover that his views on free trade are not a million miles away from those of Karl Marx. I don't know how she did it. She was the most subversive person I've ever known. But the thing I remember most about that day was her statement made at the kitchen sink where I escaped for a glass of water. 'It won't last,' she said. The beady eyes were mournful, and despite her views on marriage, there was no trace of malice in the words. Just a statement.

'How did you know?' I asked many years later.

'You were too good for him,' she said, patting my head in passing (always the head, you see?).

'He had a better degree,' I countered. 'And came from a better family.'

Beattie's almost-raucous laugh as she poured another glass of whisky (she was a well-controlled alcoholic). 'You were stronger than Andrew,' she said. 'He was bound to find out. What would he do when he did?'

The tutorial question. I wasn't falling for it.

'Try to diminish you,' she answered herself. 'What's the easiest way of doing that?'

'Pass.'

'Persuade you to have children.'

I wasn't convinced, even then. I'd always thought Andrew superior. I never did understand why he was attracted to me.

'You looked like an odalisque, snoozing in the grass,' he

20

said a few months after the Aldermaston when we'd just woken up from snoozing in his bed.

An odalisque. Now this was an improvement. All my life I've been regarded as an earth mother because of my size. I used to play up to it, wearing kaftans when they came into fashion, cooking bountiful meals, providing the cried-upon shoulder. Andrew changed all that – though it took some time. Out of a large plain quiet female he gradually fashioned a Juno, a sensual woman of mystery, an odalisque. Of course I was grateful to him. Still am.

6

We went to Scotland for our honeymoon and *en route* stopped at the Yorkshire market town where I now live. We knew instantly it was for us. The area's riddled with minor public schools of the sort chosen by families with more money than brain, so Andrew had no difficulty getting a job. Neither did I. Librarians were scarce in those days and when the Assistant Librarian retired to have a baby a few months after we arrived, they were grateful to have a qualified replacement just waiting to take over. And when, a few years later, the Chief Librarian moved south, I was his obvious successor.

Ours is quite a large library serving not only this town but several part-time branches in smaller towns and villages. We also have a mobile library which goes to remote hamlets. As Chief Librarian, I'm in charge of it all and answerable only to the County Librarian, a very competent and civilized woman who gives me considerable autonomy.

I love my job. I didn't always. Librarianship tends to attract quiet bookish types like me who are horrified to discover that libraries are not about books but people. Most never recover and become the sour snappish ladies of cartoons. I adapted and even at my first job (in London) came to like my borrowers.

I've grown fond of my regulars here, too. There's old Mr Hayes who reads nothing but sea stories because he spent his whole life at sea on the trawlers. Then there's old Mr

Ramsbottom who reads nothing but sea stories because he's never seen the sea – he's afraid to in case it disappoints him. When they run out of adult sea stories, they ransack the Children's Room. Deaf Mr Lovett wears a heavy winter overcoat in all weather – even the summer of '76 – and carries a pile of yellowed newspapers; every day he comes to his usual table, sorts through them, puts them back in order, and leaves. Mrs West carries an enormous suitcase in which she puts the one book (Goethe's poetry in German) that she takes out week after week. Mrs Coulter brings her walkie-talkie (a wired-up tin can) and converses with Martians; she used to disturb the others till I fitted an 'adaptor' so she could converse more quietly.

Not all our people are so eccentric, of course, or so nice – when I started I spent a lot of time with the mobile and, believe me, farmers are the worst. But even the grumps have their interest, and occasionally I get through to one or two. Andrew used to be amazed at some of the stories I brought home. I think he was a little jealous – children make for duller anecdotes, whatever their parents think.

We lived in a cramped flat above our butcher's for the first six months while the builder worked on our house. We did a lot of the work ourselves, weekends, but even so we couldn't have afforded it if Beattie hadn't given us an interest-free loan for the downpayment. She also gave us the better secondhand furniture and of course the rug. I wondered at the time if she was making amends for her wedding day prediction. She seemed to be trying to make things easy for us. She seldom visited – Andrew didn't really like her – but we talked a lot on the phone. I was on the phone to her the day the first of the other people's children arrived.

7

Gillian had married a year before us and lost no time in producing Sara. The co-producer, Des, was tall and pale with a pointy nose and prematurely receding hair. The description doesn't do him justice; he was quite nice looking and much more interesting than one would expect an industrial chemist to be.

Des worked near London and as both sets of parents lived within dropping-in distance Sara was much visited and spoiled. At first Gillian liked the attention but after a while she began to wonder whose child is this anyway? To placate her Des took a week off work and they headed north to a friend in Edinburgh. We were the overnight stop.

The funny thing was, the Edinburgh friend was a career-woman who didn't have any children either and lived in equally cramped quarters. I commented on this to Beattie.

'So what's so funny?' She was clearly in one of her tetchy moods.

'You'd think they'd be more sensitive,' I said.

Beattie snorted.

'Andrew explained to them,' I went on. 'He described our house in detail, said there was barely room for two visitors, let alone a child.'

The clink of ice on glass.

'Gillian just said, "No problem – Sara has her own cot.

24

We'll bring it with us." Andrew pointed out that the mattress is wall to wall, there's no room for a cot. "Never mind," said Gillian, "we'll think of something."'

There was an ominous silence. Then, 'Phyllis used to dump you and Camille on me and go off on shopping sprees.' Pause. 'I lived in a broom cupboard the landlord called a bedsit.' Pause. 'I was trying to write my thesis.'

'Beattie?' I said.

'Yes?'

'That paper you're giving at Easter – how's it going?'

'I'm writing it now.'

'I'm sorry. I'll ring off.'

And did. I knew she'd phone back later and apologize. She had an old-fashioned horror of going to bed on bad feelings in case one of us died in the night. It was the only thing she and Mummy had in common.

I was dreading the visit, less because of Sara than Andrew's antagonism towards young children. I rejoined him in our bedroom. He was glowering at the clean sheets I'd got out to put on our bed – it was obvious that the only room big enough for the three of them was ours. I stripped the bedspread and blankets and our own sheets.

'I detest one-year-olds,' said Andrew.

I agreed but said nothing. There was no point aggravating the situation.

'They crawl all over everything,' he said.

The sheets billowed out and exuded a smell of soap which momentarily cancelled the paint. (We'd only been in the house a week and it still smelled raw.)

'And knock things over,' he muttered, moving an Etruscan statue to a higher shelf though there was no way Sara could reach it anyway.

I tucked the bottom in and unfolded the first blanket.

'And stick their gooey fingers into everything,' he continued, lifting a pile of journals from the floor. They'd already been moved from the floor of his study where our mattress was to go. He looked so helpless. I pointed to the desk which we'd brought in and shoved in a corner. It was heaped with other things from the study floor but the wastepaper basket was empty. Andrew stuffed the journals in it. I winced at the symbolism. Andrew stared at the carpet. 'I suppose she'll shit on the carpet.'

'They wear nappies.'

'Nappies come off.'

'Andrew, stop being so paranoid. Come and help me with the bedspread.'

He smoothed the spread over the pillows with exaggerated care. 'I hope this will be to her majesty's satisfaction.'

I started dragging the foam mattresses out from under the bed. 'Andrew, she is your sister.'

'And you are my wife. And that' – he pointed dramatically at the mattress I was manoeuvring out of the door – 'is too soft for a decent fuck.'

I laughed and dropped the mattress and ran across and put my arms around Andrew. Magic. I kissed his Adam's apple. 'Go make me a drink,' I said.

The door opened, letting in a gust of exhaust fumes and wet earth – it was early March and raining.

'Holly!'

'Gillian!'

'Andrew!'

'Des!'

As if we were amazed at finding each other there. Gillian kissed us passionately – they were a great family for kissing – and stood back to inspect us. 'Well, how are you all?'

'Fine,' I said. 'How was your trip?'

'Awful!' said Gillian. 'Pissing with rain the whole way and Des nearly pranged a Porsche trying to over-take!'

'Who was trying—'

'Des! The idiot!'

I looked at Des. A secret demon driver? He did seem rather strained. 'Never mind,' I said. 'You're here now. Look, why don't we get the things out of the car and then you can park in the lane around the corner – there's a restriction on—'

'Great!'

I never got used to the way Gillian greeted every piece of information with uniform ecstasy.

We stood by the car in the damp dusk while Des hauled out a cot, blankets, toys, suitcases, kitchen things, cardboard boxes. It looked like they were staying a month.

Gillian intercepted a look between Andrew and me and laughed. 'Isn't it awful? You know what it's like with kids!'

'Yes,' I said, though I didn't.

We piled the things inside and shut the door. Sara had found her way to the scuttle and was trying to eat a lump of coal.

'Put it down, Sweetie,' said Gillian.

It dropped onto the chair nearest the fire. Andrew picked it up and put it back in the scuttle. He wiped the coal dust from the chair, leaving a black smudge.

'Never mind,' I said. 'It's an old chair.'

Gillian hadn't noticed. She'd picked up one of my alabaster jars. 'How sweet! I didn't know you collected!'

It sounded like a disease. 'Not seriously.'

Andrew and Des were taking the luggage upstairs. It took two trips each and left me alone with Gillian. I always felt nervous with Gillian. Her effusiveness seemed to diminish the lives of those around her. She put the jar down on the perspex top of the record deck and scanned the room. 'How sweet! It must be incredibly cosy in blizzards! You have a lot of blizzards!'

It seemed pointless to contradict.

'Let me get you a drink,' I said.

'Super! A very dry sherry?'

I poured one out and handed it to her.

'Lovely!' She set it down on the record deck and put her hands on her knees. 'Sara Sweetie! Come and say hello to Auntie Holly and say how marvellous it is to be here!'

Sara chortled – she was a very friendly child – and made her way towards us along the perimeter of the room, clutching everything on the way for support. She clutched the record deck. I lunged but too late. Sherry dribbled over the *Eroica*. The alabaster jar teetered and fell.

'Oh my God!' Gillian picked up a fragment of alabaster. 'I hope it wasn't valuable!'

'No,' I said.

'Shouldn't she be in bed?' said Andrew.

We were all in the kitchen. Des and Gillian were sitting at the table with their drinks. I was tossing a salad. Andrew was by the cooker folding in the last ingredient of a French thing he hadn't made before. Sara was climbing up his leg.

'She's much too excited to go to bed, aren't you, Sweetie?'

Des had been talking about whether a hypodermic needle would work for spot weed-killing. I was very interested – gardening links the most unlikely people – but hadn't been able to follow very well because Sara was babbling and screeching so.

Andrew shook her off to put his dish in the oven. I heard a soft plop as her behind hit the lino. Her face crumpled up. I attracted her attention by clicking my tongue and then made an inane face to divert the howl. It worked, but she screamed with laughter instead and my ears were no better off. She started up his leg again.

'Will someone please remove this praying mantis from my leg?' said Andrew.

'Come over here and stop bothering your uncle. He's busy.'

The edge in Gillian's voice matched Andrew's. I washed my hands quickly and detached Sara. I didn't know much about children but I'd seen other people jiggle them up and down so I tried that.

'She adores you!' cried Gillian.

A smell was rising from the vicinity of Sara's nappy. 'I think she needs changing,' I said.

'Oh, Lord, yes, I'd forgotten!' Gillian got up and took her from me.

'*Now?*' said Andrew. He looked at the timer he'd set.

'I won't be two ticks!' She disappeared upstairs with Sara.

The kitchen was silent except for the timer. Des cleared his throat. 'The main problem as I see it,' he said, 'is how to prevent the needle from clogging up with vegetable matter. Plants are so much squishier than humans.'

Fifteen minutes later, mother and daughter reappeared, clean and fresh, just as the timer went ping. Andrew seemed relieved. He hadn't seen the tin of baby food Gillian was clutching.

'*Now?*' he said, when he did see it.

'She'll just get grisly if I don't.'

The thought of all that energy gone grisly was enough for me, but Andrew persisted. 'It's like a soufflé. It'll flop.'

'Oh, don't mind me,' said Gillian brightly. 'Just leave my bit in the oven.'

We had to serve up anyway – the only saucepan suitable for warming up Sara's dinner was the one containing my leeks in cream sauce. I washed it up, handed it to Gillian, and prepared for a dinner *à trois*. But earth mothers – even retired ones – aren't like that. We can't relax while someone else is bustling around untaken-care-of. I popped up to fetch Sara's special bowl and spoon. I popped up to detach Sara from Andrew's leg again – she was crawling around under the table. I popped up to bring Gillian a glass of wine at the cooker.

At last we were *à cinq*, Sara enthroned on Gillian's lap, her face smeared with orange goo and beaming across the table at me. I smiled back – people always smile at children, regardless of what they feel. The orange mouth opened and a stream of sick poured out.

We were in the living room. Sara had been coaxed into her cot at last, and the four of us were having a reasonably intelligent conversation about the art treasures ruined by the Florence floods and whether money should be spent on them or on the poor in Italy. Gillian wasn't contributing much. She'd been wearing a Mona Lisa smile all evening. Finally Andrew noticed.

'What are you smirking at?'

'Don't I have a charming brother?' said Gillian. 'Thank God he married you instead of some creep like himself.'

'Well, you were smirking,' I said.

The smirk returned. There was a pregnant pause. Very pregnant. 'Des and I are having another baby,' she announced.

No wonder Des had nearly pranged a Porsche. 'How nice,' I said. I was wondering where the second cot would go on future visits. And a third? I saw our bedroom turned into one of those hospital showrooms with rows of red faces peered at through a picture window.

'What's wrong with Sara?' said Andrew.

Gillian didn't understand.

'She seems all right to me,' he said.

Gillian still didn't understand, though she ought to have known his views on children by then.

'He means that most people have a second baby because they make a mess of the first,' I explained. I felt like one of those awful wives who translate for their disabled husbands as if they aren't there. Andrew was only disabled by wine. 'Sara's such a sweet-natured child,' I added. 'It does seem a shame to risk getting a grotty one next time around.'

Gillian found this very amusing.

Des was more serious. 'Perhaps you're right,' he said. 'But it would be terrible to make Sara an only child.' He made it sound like a disease even worse than collecting alabaster jars.

The phone rang. I looked at the grandfather clock, picked up the receiver and said, 'Hello Beattie.'

A startled silence at the other end. Then, 'How did you know it was me?'

I laughed. 'I'm sorry I interrupted your writing,' I said.

'That's all right. Actually, I phoned to say I'm sorry I was so grisly.'

Grisly. I saw a tiny red-faced Beattie at a hospital picture window and was shocked. Beattie a baby? No doubt my well-meaning grandmother had produced my mother to save Beattie from the disease of only-childness.

'How's it going?' I asked.

'It seems rather brilliant at the moment. What it'll look like tomorrow morning is another matter. Holly, you asked me a question.'

'Did I?' I heard the click of a lighter – as well as being an alcoholic, Beattie smoked – and knew she was settling in for a long chat.

'About why people with children prey on the childless.'

'I'm sure I didn't say that.'

'Well, more or less. Think about it.' She left the tutorial

pause and when I didn't reply – I never was very good in tutorials – supplied the answer herself. 'Because they can't retaliate. Nobody really likes other people's children. Not even parents.'

We were too tired to make love that night. I expect Des was, too. The only one of us who seemed to have any energy left was Gillian. I pondered this for some time. I'd always heard motherhood was so exhausting, but Gillian seemed to feed on it. Perhaps (I thought subversively) she was feeding on the rest of us, using up our energy while conserving her own. I remembered Beattie's comment. It was certainly true of me. I'd never much liked other people's children. I'd assumed therefore that I wouldn't like my own either, but other people didn't seem to feel that way – I mean the other people who eventually produced children of their own. Suddenly a shocking thought came to me: perhaps people had children as revenge. Perhaps after years of being imposed on by other people's children, they produced some of their own to impose on the people who had imposed on them. You're drunk (I told myself). It's natural to want children. You're the one who's unnatural. I pushed the subject away and took my mind out into the garden. There was a laburnum I was planning to chuck out and replace with a magnolia. It was a risky choice for up here, and there'd be no flowers for maybe ten years. In ten years I'd be thirty-four. Sara would be eleven, working for her Eleven Plus. Andrew might be a headmaster. I might be Chief Librarian. The magnolia would be flowering. In the dark behind my eyes I created it, cell by cell, twig by twig, watched it branch out and up into the grey sky, and then one day walked out into the garden to see the first flower buds . . .

'Holly?'

I awoke in a panic: I'd overslept, my guests were looking for their breakfast. But the curtainless window was dark and the watch by the mattress said 2.45. I'd been asleep half an hour.

'Holly?'

The door opened two inches before bumping into the mattress. In the brightly lighted slit stood a portion of Gillian. 'Sorry to be such a drag, but do you have any Vicks Vapo-Rub? Sara's all clogged up. I think it's the fresh paint.' Gillian moved to reveal part of a wheezing Sara.

'I don't think so.'

'Oh God, the one thing I didn't pack!' There was a cosmic helplessness about her that Andrew sometimes shared – as if the whole world had suddenly collapsed on their head. I put on my dressing gown, eased a corner of the mattress up, and squeezed through the doorway. 'I'll see what I can find.'

'You really are an angel!'

I didn't feel very angelic. I was doing my Saturday tomorrow and on top of that we were stock-taking.

'Andrew says you know all about herbs,' said Gillian hopefully.

I nodded, too tired to speak. It wasn't true. The only thing I knew was how to grow them, but one of my old gardening books had a section on uses. I took it down from the shelf while Gillian sat by the banked-up fire. 'Asthma?' I suggested.

Gillian looked alarmed.

'Bronchitis?'

'Good God no! Isn't there something for Stuffed Up Nose?'

I looked under Nose and Stuffed. 'I think you need a medical term.'

'Try Asthma, then.'

'*Elder, elecampane, garlic, heartsease, honeysuckle, hore-*

hound, mullein, plantain, poppy, speedwell, vervain, yarrow,'
I read out.

'Do you have any of those?'

'Only garlic.'

'She wouldn't take it.'

'It's March, Gillian. There's nothing growing.'

The cosmic helplessness.

I tried to remember if plantain died back in winter. 'Possibly plantain,' I suggested.

'Would you mind terribly having a look?'

It was raining. Sara wheezed again. We went to the kitchen and I put on my wellies and raincoat and hat. I felt a right fool. Even if the plantain was there, the infusion would take ages and Sara would almost certainly refuse to drink it. If she did drink it it wouldn't do any good. I knew perfectly well I'd end up jammed into a chair by the banked-up fire while Gillian and Sara stretched out on the sofa and finally fell asleep between wheezes and I'd wake up stiff and bleary without knowing I'd slept and I'd make breakfast for us all before going off to be nice to grumpy borrowers and a week later the whole scene would be played again when Gillian and Des and Sara stayed here on their way back from Scotland. So why was I standing at the back door dressed up like old Mr Hayes from the library about to join his trawler? To ward off the cosmic helplessness, that's why. I looked at Gillian. She seemed more Brünhilde-ish than ever with her long blonde hair tumbling over her long white dressing gown. She seemed as fresh as she had when she arrived. I imagined her giving a great 'Ho yo to ho!' and galloping off into battle to snatch up the day's quota of dead warriors. Instead, she moved nearer the door and said, 'You really are marvellous, Holly. I feel dreadful imposing on you like this.' Then she smiled as if she'd suddenly had a brilliant idea. She put her hand on my arm and gave me a conspiratorial look. 'I'll work on Andrew,' she whispered, though there was no one there to hear except Sara, 'and then when you have your kids, you can come and impose on us!'

8

My unsuccessful search for plantain is as good an excuse as any to describe the garden. But it was dark and rainy that night, and the garden bore little resemblance then to what it is now. As with the house, it's difficult to know which part of its seventeen years with me to describe. The house began well and rapidly declined; the garden began as an imitation of its 'big house' Edwardian models and turned into Eden.

I think I've already said that one of my predecessors bought the land adjacent, thus turning a long narrow strip into a large square (the house takes up only one corner). It's a third of an acre but seems much larger because the curving paths never let you see beyond the next bend. In addition, my predecessor (as cunning as I) left gaps in the back hedge through which the woodland beyond is visually annexed to the garden. It's a standard trick, of course.

And the hedge? Roses: wild, old-fashioned, most of them fragrant, more a screen than a hedge. Five feet wide and six to eight feet high, it's a fairy ring to me and a high-density housing complex to the hundreds of birds who live in my garden. Nor is this the only housing; my garden is a dense mass of trees and shrubs which threaten to close up the paths. There are open areas, too, with herbaceous plants and alpines, though there is no rockery – I hate those arid places that look dusty even in downpours. I also hate lupins, tulips, pink flowering cherries, laburnums, monkey puzzle trees, and those stiff triangular dwarf conifers bred to a gaudy gold or blue. I hate beds cut into lawns. Come to that, I don't much like lawns either. I have only a small one of chamomile on which I daydream and drink Cinzano and make love with my boyfriend Barnaby and sometimes all three together.

When Andrew and I came here the garden was a dizzy jigsaw of lawns and beds and borders booby-trapped with pergolas and urns. There were rustic seats at every turn. There was a goldfish pond. I did nothing for a year except replace a laburnum with a magnolia. I watched the garden, studied it, made hundreds of diagrams and lists. Then I got going. Even so, it was a gradual change, and few things of substance have gone. The shrubberies and borders just grew, eating away at the lawns till nothing was left of them but a few winding grassy paths. When I replaced the last lawn with chamomile, I converted the paths to stone paving and sold the mower. The goldfish pond now houses frogs. I once spent a chilly night in the treehouse Des built for his son, just so I could listen to the spring courtship.

Yes, it's a very natural garden — people always say so. They mean it as a compliment and are surprised when I frown and say, 'What is this "natural"?' They've never thought about the poor abused word, nor about its companion, 'life'.

I abuse these words myself when it suits me. Some kind soul who wanted to rehabilitate my reputation tipped off the BBC and I was asked to take part in a series they were doing on ordinary people's gardens. I could see it all: the write-up in the local paper, dozens of people trying to peer through the hedge, a few brave ones knocking at the door and asking, so sweetly and politely, if they might just have a little look around . . . It was mean of me to refuse, but I'd shared too much of my life with too many people too long. I was extremely apologetic on the phone. 'Well,' I said

shyly, 'it's sort of a *nature* reserve, a *wildlife* sanctuary ...'
'I understand,' said the producer, or perhaps it was a secretary.

In one sense my garden is a third of an acre; in another, it's eight hundred and fifty. The west (back) boundary gives on to an estate owned by the most amiable of our three local squires. Except in the shooting and breeding seasons I have access to all of it. I'm on good terms with the estate workers. There's a regular exchange of cuttings. I collect casual firewood from his land. I dig up the wildlings that sow themselves in my soft borders and with his blessing I return them to his wood. Barnaby sneers at my underplanting service but I point out that my squire is death duty weakened and works on a shoestring, though a squire's shoestring is longer than ours. I know the squire's motives are mixed, that my walks through his woods benefit him by keeping at bay the deer that are moving down from Scotland and threatening us all. So? Squires are easy targets. I'm more concerned with people who go unexamined and unqueried through an easy and natural life.

Mummy was one of the first to join Life. It was, she said, a natural extension of her love of plants. I love plants too but am opposed to Life. 'All life is one,' she said in her mystical voice. 'Slugs too?' I said, but she didn't understand. She's not even vegetarian.

Mummy and Beattie drifted further apart when Beattie joined the Voluntary Euthanasia Society. Mummy was horrified. 'Life is God's gift,' she said, 'His to give and His to take away.' 'Then God's an Indian-giver,' said Beattie, 'and I may as well choose my own time and place.'

So there it is: Mummy the heroine of the life-force, Beattie the villain of the death-wish, and my garden and mind the battleground. Eden was symbolic too.

9

Our contemporaries were marrying at such a rapid rate that
Andrew and I seemed to spend every weekend travelling
somewhere for someone's wedding, and in June 1967, just
a few months after the Sara episode, it was Camille's turn.

This time Mummy had her way: the pretty church, the
hopeful hymns, the flowers, bridesmaids, even Men-
delssohn. She failed with the wedding gown, though. I
remember her on the morning, when it was too late anyway,
staring miserably at Camille's white satin mini dress. 'Think
of the photographs! You'll be sorry, ten years from now . . .'
(She was.)

At least Camille had the sense to keep it simple. As I've
said, beauty is not our strong point, but with a little crafty
make-up and her dark curly hair, she looked extremely
pretty. A fussy dress and veil would have ruined it.

I hesitate to describe the groom. Perhaps everyone who
has a well-loved sister feels she should have done better,
but Camille's husband was a type I particularly dislike: the
wiry little health freak who jogs and has a beard and is
always called Mike, and yes, his name was Mike. Though
my own vices are few and mild, I always feel nervous around
those who have none. Mike didn't smoke, drank only beer
and then moderately, ate food high in fibre and low in fat,
did push-ups every morning, and belonged to Friends of
the Earth. Really, he was a model human, and so good-
natured I feel awful talking about him like this. Everyone

else adored him – he's the kind of person everyone wants their daughter to marry. Beattie and I were the odd ones out. Once again I fled to the sink for a glass of water. Beattie was there already. 'It won't last,' she said.

They honeymooned in Scotland and stayed with us on their way back. It was a lovely visit, despite the early-morning grunts of Mike doing his push-ups. All that energy. 'What's wrong with sex?' said Andrew, echoing my own views.

Camille had stayed with us before, and though she liked the town, she was very much a city girl. Now, however, she saw it double, through Mike's eyes as well, and what had previously been 'pleasant' became 'marvellous'. I suppose it's a healthy town.

In September they moved up here. I was delighted. I had friends enough from school and university and my two years in London, but none had ever displaced Camille. I think she felt the same. I pictured the long winter evenings spent over a groaning dinner table, the easy-going rambles in the countryside, the odd-jobs we would do for each other, and above all, the long long talks.

Mike had no difficulty finding a job – he was, of course, a PE teacher. Camille had to wait longer. There's not much call for social workers in our area.

They lived in the same flat above the butcher's while the same builder (Barnaby) worked on their house: Ryegill, a derelict hill farm several miles out the other side of town. They had an acre of tatty land which Camille, while waiting for a job, turned into a miniature smallholding with a large vegetable garden, a goat, hens, and a trio of the most bad-tempered geese I've ever met. This was all in advance of the self-sufficiency fad which came in the '70s; by then Camille and Mike had installed a Franco-Belge which did the cooking and hot water and radiators, a hydraulic ram which pumped water up from their beck without using electricity, and a complicated set of compost heaps. It was a marvellous place to be. Even Andrew thought so. We spent most of our weekends (when not attending weddings) working up there. It never seemed like work; the jobs that needed doing were always odd and exotic, not like unblocking sinks and repapering bathrooms and all the tedious things that happen in town houses. Looking back I see four children playing at Utopia. The only time Camille seemed dissatisfied was during those few months of 1968 when the students of Europe were suddenly in earnest and rioting all over the place. 'I feel like a traitor,' she said to me one day as we earthed up the spuds in her rural idyll. What could I say? She was right.

10

Paint my garden green. The yellow days of forsythia are over, the pink of the roses is yet to come. In between, a tender green interlude as leaf buds open and trees turn into summer parasols.

I'm feeling rather lyrical, kneeling by the cold frame and pricking out parsley. I should have done it weeks ago.

A bluetit is swinging from a strip of gammon rind tied on a feeder near the kitchen. He's completely horizontal and seems to have fallen asleep. There are other feeders in private places for those who don't like an audience, but extroverts are encouraged to perform for my pleasure.

I put the little pots of parsley back in the frame to harden off. A sharp 'CHIT!' sounds and I look up, though I already know what I'll see: the resident great spotted woodpecker zooming in to scare the hell out of the bluetit. I'd flee, too; that thing's got a beak on it like a sword.

'Can't you share?' I say. 'There's plenty for all.'

The woodpecker drives his beak into the block of fat he's claimed for his own.

11

Mummy and Daddy usually stayed at Ryegill when they came north. Mummy preferred the comfort of our house, but Daddy said Andrew and I both had full-time jobs and couldn't be expected to do them well after spending the night crammed in the boxroom. Camille had three spare bedrooms and all the time in the world for visitors.

It was true, of course, but Daddy also liked pottering about at Ryegill. The hydraulic ram, for example, was his idea. He drew up the plans, searched out the components and put it together himself. Mummy found this all very boring and deplored the lack of flowers. She always brought a carload of her surplus to plant out in the weedy remains of what had been a proper old cottage garden, but Camille ignored them and they usually died. Finally Mummy gave up and, while Daddy made himself useful at Ryegill, pottered about in my garden instead.

Patterns again. It was as if Camille and I were each, briefly, trying to woo the parent that least liked us: me with my flowers and Camille with her technical projects. It didn't work, my mother and I could never be close – we had nothing in common but gardens. Still, in those first three years of Ryegill, we all came as near as we ever would to being a perfect family.

A composite picture then. I choose a summer day. As in the childhood memories, it's forever warm and sunny. We're at the back of the house, on the acre of rough grass which today is playing the role of hayfield. Daddy crouches over the big mower Mike's hired for the weekend. Like all hired machinery it's rebelled against multiple ownership and broken down halfway through the job. Daddy sympathizes with this hunk of dirty metal. His ministrations are gentle, though sweat drips off his brow and necessitates frequent recourse to the bottle of Theakstons propped against a hummock of grass. The undershirt which Mummy allows him only at Ryegill shows dark stains where the sweat has made a river bed of his body.

Mummy is wearing the gaily flowered cotton dress she calls her peasant costume – like the undershirt, it's reserved for Ryegill. She's tied her hair off her forehead with a colourful scarf and is leaning against a big wooden hayrake. The role of rustic suits her more than you'd think. Someone should take a photograph but doesn't. The weather's so hot that the section mown yesterday is ready for turning. This she does with long expert strokes though to the best of my knowledge she was never a landgirl.

Andrew and Mike are stripped to the waist. They're building a hut for the geese, one of which was killed last week by a neighbour's sheepdog. The gander and his remaining mate are not far off, keeping an eye on things while tugging at the grass with short angry motions which suggest displacement. They've got a nerve. This whole Millais scene is being done for their benefit so that they (and the goat) have hay for the long lean winter.

Camille, in shorts and a checked shirt tied in a knot under her bra, is painting a windowframe. The smell of paint and the smell of mown grass compete for centre-stage. A cat winds itself around her leg and suffers a blob of paint on its head. Camille wipes it off but the cat is offended and moves on.

I, reverting to my role of earth mother, am sitting by the back door shelling peas which I may as well admit are store-bought; Camille's are still in flower – we have short growing seasons up here.

The phone rings. Camille puts down her paintbrush and goes into the grey stone house to answer it. The heavy oak door thuds shut. Daddy looks up. He sees a white clapboard farmhouse and hears the gentler thud of a screen door. On days like this his accent is stronger.

Camille returns and says who it was, but we don't hear anything because this is a soundtrack without words. Families don't function through words. Looks, gestures, laughter at an old shared joke – this is the language of families. But we're in the 1960s and silent films are out, so I supply a few details for verisimilitude: sheep bleating on the hills further up, the grumpy chit-chat of geese, the clink of nuts and bolts as Daddy places them carefully on a scrap of old metal at his side, the banging of Mike's hammer, the swish of Camille's paintbrush, the gentle pop of peas falling into a saucepan. Only Mummy is silent. She's leaning on her rake again, watching Camille. Mummy's opted out of the golden age and allowed dissatisfaction to furrow her pretty face. Something is missing in Arcadia.

Mummy wants grandchildren.

12

Some three years after she married, Camille obliged. She'd never made a secret of her view that a marriage without children was a nonsense, but I was surprised at the timing. After a year unemployed, she'd finally got a toehold in the social services with a part-time job and a year later gone full-time. Camille is one of those compulsively active people who thinks an evening spent reading is an evening wasted; when she runs out of legitimate work, she invents tasks for herself. These usually involve other people as well, so her job was a blessing to us all.

Then she had Emma. I assumed she would stop work till Emma started school. No. She was by then entitled to, and took, a substantial maternity leave (I like to think this was not calculation on her part) with her job left open at the end of it. When the time came for her to return, she found a professional child-minder for three days a week and a friend for the fourth. That left one.

'It all seems very complicated,' I said to her when she dropped in for coffee on my day off. 'Wouldn't it be easier just to work part-time?'

'We need the money,' she said.

I suppose it was true. Though their house had been derelict and cheap, and though Mummy had given them the financial assistance Beattie gave us, it was still a fairly big mortgage.

'Anyway,' she added, 'I'd go up the wall if I didn't get out of the house every day.'

It seemed a sad comment on Emma, lying peacefully in her pram by the kitchen table. 'Couldn't you get together with some other mothers and work out a rota?'

'I'd have to be on it,' she reminded me.

Emma moved as if thinking of waking up. Camille didn't see her. She was gazing glumly into her coffee like a soap-opera heroine. Come to think of it, it was rather like one of those *kaffeeklatsch* scenes.

YOUNG MOTHER (*looking up suddenly with a gleam of new hope*): I don't suppose you could take her on your day off . . .

CAREER WOMAN (*laughs*): Me? I don't know one end of a baby from the other!

YOUNG MOTHER (*animated*): It's dead easy, Holly. I'll show you what to do. She's such a good baby, she just sleeps in her pram all day and –

CAREER WOMAN (*frowning*): Camille, you know it's my gardening day. God knows I have little enough time as it is and –

YOUNG MOTHER (*jumps up excitedly*): Oh, just put the pram in the garden, she loves being in the fresh air! You will do it, Holly, won't you, please, I'm counting on you . . .

(*Focus on* CAREER WOMAN's *face as it turns from horror to despair to . . . resignation. Cut.*)

This day off. It's not a gift but exchange for evening and weekend work; i.e. Sunday is the only other day I can get into the garden.

'Garden!' Camille exploded when several weeks later I complained of my surrogate motherhood (Emma did *not* sleep in her pram all day). 'That's all you ever think about is a bunch of mouldy old plants! Emma's a *living human being*!'

Living. Life. But I didn't have time to reply.

'So's Holly!' Andrew shouted back. 'And she's a nervous wreck looking after that brat! If we wanted kids we'd have them ourselves!'

It was Andrew who had started the row, and though I appreciated his taking my side I was almost too shocked to notice. Camille and I hadn't rowed since we were kids and never so seriously.

'I don't suppose *you* could learn to change a nappy!' she yelled at Andrew. 'Or is that too demeaning for a public school teacher!'

'Camille, that's unfair,' I said. 'You know he isn't here half the time.' Andrew spent much of the summer as a courier for a Roman-ruins-in-Britain company.

'No, he's screwing the tourists for lots of lovely money so you can live like fat bourgeois pigs!'

'I'd rather be a bourgeois pig than a phoney hippie!' Andrew shouted.

'WILL YOU TWO SHUT UP!'

They shut up.

'Look,' I said, 'I'm sorry I said anything. I don't mind having Emma, really I don't. It's no trouble at all.' I made myself smile. 'No trouble at all.'

13

I wheeled the pram through the library doors, past the issue
desk, down along the rows of shelves, and into the staffroom.
I parked it by the sink and set the big wicker basket of
Emmaiana beside it. Mr McDonald sidled out of his office.
He peered into the pram.

'What, may I ask, is this?'

Mr McDonald was a tall angular Scot of the generation
which worked at losing its accent and cultivated a facetious
turn of phrase.

'A baby, I believe,' I said, trying for a lighthearted tone.
'My niece, actually. Mr McDonald, Emma; Emma, Mr
McDonald.'

For a moment I thought it had worked. 'And how long
are we to have the pleasure of Miss Emma's company?'

'Only for the day.'

'The *whole* day?'

My heart, as they say in novels, sank. I tried taking him
into my confidence. 'I'm as sorry about this as you are,' I
said. 'The girl who usually looks after her went down with
'flu and Camille just turned up on the doorstep this morning.
I told her it was out of the question but she drove off and
what was I to do, just leave the pram parked in front of an
empty house all day? I could hardly do that, could I?'

Mr McDonald looked as if he thought I could.

'Really, she's no trouble,' I said. 'She just sleeps in her
pram all day.'

Trouble-free Emma squirmed under the blanket and screwed up her face for a yell. Mr McDonald took off his glasses and rubbed his eyes with the back of his hand, a well-known danger signal.

'You're quite sure this is a single, solitary, isolated occasion?' he said.

'Oh yes, definitely!'

'And if your sister leaves the pram on your doorstep tomorrow morning?'

'Out of the question – Mrs Sproat has her tomorrow.'

'And if Mrs Sproat acquires the 'flu?'

He raised a facetious eyebrow and sidled back into his office, leaving a swarm of question marks dancing around my head. Chief among them was promotion. I knew he'd applied for a job down south. If he got it, I was next in line for his. I don't want to sound like a power hungry book-monger, but I dearly wanted that job – quite apart from the humiliation of being passed over and having to adapt to a new and no doubt younger male superior.

It was the worst Emma-day I'd had so far. Emma screamed, cried, spewed and shat non-stop. I inspected for thistles in her nappy and foreign objects in her throat. Not a thing. The cause of Emma's angst was clearly emotional, and about that I could do nothing. The only respite we had was during the coffee and tea breaks when some of the part-timers – mothers themselves – picked her up and mysteriously silenced her with whatever magic mothers possess. For the rest, I opened the windows wide to disperse into the rainy air the 'aural and olefactory evidence of Miss Emma's distress', as Mr McDonald put it.

By the end of the day I was (a) exhausted, and (b) convinced I'd lost not only the chance of promotion but my present job as well. I fled to the issue desk, hoping for a little comfort from the familiar faces of my regulars. There weren't many. It was the height of the tourist season, when the early-summer flood of families with pre-schoolers gives way to the late-summer deluge of families with schoolchildren. Children children children. The world seemed packed full of them with only a handful of harassed adults standing between them and total anarchy. I counted up the temporary tickets issued to children that day alone and was horrified though it was all to the good as far as the annual report was concerned. No wonder my regulars were staying away in droves. Only deaf old Mr Lovett remained, serenely sorting his newspapers in his usual corner. I beamed a smile of peace into his oblivious back and went into the storeroom behind the desk to set up the overdue notice machine.

When I returned, a young woman was standing at the desk grinning at me. She was wearing a soggy denim jacket, a bright red shirt, and an even brighter head of frizzy ginger hair. Her face was round and moon-like, with flat freckled cheeks. She looked vaguely familiar but I'd never seen her before. I prepared to be friendly to a tourist.

'Holly?' she said.

I was startled at first, then remembered the name plate on the desk. Even so, it was odd. We're a bit old-fashioned in this town. I nodded pleasantly.

'Hi!' she said. 'I'm your cousin Alice!'

'Good heavens,' I said. I'd always known I had American cousins but I never expected to see any of them. When Daddy stopped flying he lost touch, letters being a poor substitute for presence and Daddy being a reluctant correspondent anyway. Without thinking, I leaned over the desk. Two large duffle bags but no babies. 'Good heavens,' I repeated, this time with a smile.

She was, she announced, a drop-out, though that was fairly obvious from her appearance. She'd been living in a California commune but it was too squalid so 'I just packed my bags and off I went! I thought maybe you guys did these things better over here.'

I pictured a Yorkshire commune with tweed-clad dropouts perched on their shooting sticks in front of a log fire. 'I really wouldn't know,' I said 'but Camille has a lot of contacts. I'm sure she could give you some addresses.'

'Fantastic!'

It was impossible not to like Alice. Emma was screaming in the distance and a bunch of kids were tearing up the Children's Room and I was about to lose my job and into it all walked this stout little laid-back emissary of a new life. Suddenly I had a vision: merry Alice entertaining Emma while I worked in the garden. *Whole, uninterrupted, peaceful days in the garden.* I did some quick calculations: Alice wasn't at all Andrew's type so no problem there. And by now we were having so many visitors with kids that Andrew had moved his desk into the living room (there was only space for one so I'd forfeited and sold my own). That meant the boxroom was free at last and with only a single mattress, there would be just about enough room to move around. 'Look,' I said, 'Camille's place is in chaos – they're tearing it up to put in central heating – but we've got a spare room. It's only tiny, but you're welcome to stay as long as you like.'

'No kidding? Fantastic! That's really great!' She turned and called, 'Zach?' A ginger-haired little boy came running from the Children's Room. 'This is my son,' said Alice. 'Zachary, say hi to cousin Holly!'

14

We didn't go away on holiday that year – partly because of Alice (she stayed a month), partly because of Andrew's sporadic summer work. I didn't mind. I took my holiday in bits and pieces; some I used up showing Alice and Zach the local sights, the rest went on the garden. By the end of the summer it was looking pretty good, apart from a few borders persistently trampled and eaten by Zach. It's hard to discipline other people's children – they don't listen (no real sanctions) and the mothers always resent it so.

Most children have a passion for sweets; Zach had a passion for plants. You'd think the bitterness would put him off but, like a horse deprived of trace minerals and chewing fenceposts in lieu, Zach went around chewing the leaves of my plants, both indoors and out. Chewing, not swallowing; he spat out the remains. I was terrified in case some were poisonous but Alice had no such fears. 'He's been eating them since he was two,' she said, 'and look at him now!' He certainly did seem a healthy child.

Oddly enough, this wasn't so. Zach's father turned up one night and after a terrific row carted the child back to the States to resume medical treatment for some bizarre and extremely rare disease which accounted for the plant eating. Apparently Alice had objected to the treatment – she was into wholefoods and regarded all drugs except marijuana as 'unnatural' – so she'd kidnapped her own son from the clinic. The father was legally entitled to re-kidnap him, and Alice finally gave in. In fact, except for the stormy scene and a subsequent morning of tears, Alice recovered remarkably fast. She went off to a commune recommended by Camille. We didn't see her again for some years.

The following summer Andrew was adamant: we were going to Italy, to hell with anyone else. It caused a little friction with various friends who'd been hoping to stay on their way to or from Scotland, and Camille had to find someone else to do my Emma-days. But when the time came, we just locked up the house and went.

It was marvellous. We'd been married five years and spent so little of that time alone together it was like a second honeymoon. I'd almost forgotten what fun Andrew could be. In Italy he shed not only several years but also the authoritarian manner which disfigures most schoolteachers. We were young, free, and very happy.

Andrew had been before, of course, and knew many out-of-the-way places. He also had a nose for just the right little *pensione* or restaurant. His Italian was only so-so, but when he couldn't find the right word, he filled in with Latin. It seemed to amuse the locals. On the whole, they were very nice to us, though towards the end we got a little tired of the phrase '*Bambini non ci sono?*' ('No children?'), usually spoken by an ancient black-clad woman who'd clearly had heaps of her own. There *did* seem to be an awful lot of *bambini* around, and when I saw the way they ran wild I realized how much effort some of our own visitors had put into controlling theirs.

Nevertheless, opening the front door was a shock. The house had, in our absent minds, reverted to new. Seeing the reality, we saw how much it had changed. The white walls were landscaped with coally grey smudges and crayon lines. The curtain rails were bent and the curtains hanging askew from children swinging on them. Beattie's oriental rug exuded a faint odour of urine and milky vomit.

And of course, no plants. They'd disappeared one by one the previous summer so we hadn't noticed the cumulative impact till now.

I still wasn't noticing it; I was watching Andrew's face as the extra years and the authoritarian manner slid back onto it. 'Never mind,' I said. 'I was getting tired of them anyway.'

Perhaps it was true. I set about trying to convince myself. Houseplants require constant attentiveness, which, as my boyfriend Barnaby says, is different from attention. He has only one, a gigantic grape ivy, but he's forever prodding the soil and inspecting every leaf. No wonder it adores him. My time was becoming too fragmented for this kind of vigilance. 'Houseplants are unnatural,' I said to Andrew in a voice which was itself unnaturally hard. 'Plants belong outside. How many cavemen had houseplants?'

15

I went onto the Pill soon after I met Andrew. When we returned from Italy, I'd been on it six years.

'I don't think that's a good idea,' said Andrew.

Neither did I.

I went to my doctor. (There are three doctors in the surgery I attend. I had the sense to sign on with the only one who didn't have an Irish name.) 'What are the alternatives?' I asked.

He told me. One by one I tried them. My body – capacious, friendly and sound – rejected them all.

'What's left?' I asked.

'Why don't you just start your family now?'

'But we don't want a family.'

It took a long time for this to sink in. Then, 'I'm afraid I can't help you,' he said.

I went back onto the Pill.

'I don't think that's a good idea,' said Andrew.

Neither did I.

I went back to my doctor. 'Which method of sterilization do you recommend?' I asked.

'Sterilization?' Another long pause while the nature of my request registered. Then, 'I'm afraid there's no right to sterilization on the NHS.'

'But?'

'It's a complex and expensive operation,' he said. 'Unless

56

there's a good medical reason, it's a luxury the NHS can't afford.'

I knew the NHS would afford me a dozen babies if I so desired, but I said nothing. I waited it out.

Finally, 'If you're determined,' he said, 'I'll make an appointment for you with the area health authority's consultant obstetrician and gynaecologist. He'll consider your case and decide. However, I must warn you that there are risks.' He described the operation in graphic detail.

'It's clear,' I said when he finished, 'that my chances of surviving it are approximately equal to those of surviving a heart transplant.'

He laughed – I'll give him that, he had a sense of humour – 'Any operation involving a total anaesthetic is dangerous,' he said. It sounded like a threat. I took it as one.

'I don't think that's a good idea,' said Andrew when I described the operation.

Neither did I. 'I don't suppose you'd consider a vasectomy?' I said.

'ME?'

I dropped the subject for several weeks and only came back to it when Andrew seemed ready. He agreed I should at least find out more.

'Oh yes,' said my doctor when I asked. 'A very simple operation. Yes, just a local anaesthetic. Yes, very quick and cheap to do. It would only cost your husband £40.'

'Cost him?'

'He'd have to have it done privately,' he explained. 'Vasectomies are extremely rare on the NHS and not done at all in this particular area health authority. If you wish your husband to have a free vasectomy –'

'Free? After all the years we've been paying our National Insurance?'

'– if you wish to have a free vasectomy, you might wish to consider moving to Newcastle.'

'Newcastle?'

'I believe they permit free vasectomies in Newcastle.' He said the name as if he were saying Gomorrah.

'But we *have* paid,' I said. 'All these years paying for other people to have their children, surely we should get a little something out of it ourselves—'

'You don't expect to "get a little something" out of your house insurance, do you? It's there in case the radiators leak and ruin your carpets.'

I considered this a moment. 'I am not a radiator,' I said quietly.

He laughed.

16

It was about this time that Beattie made one of her rare visits to us. She'd just come back from a conference in Leipzig and I was fascinated by what she had to report. Not the conference – even Beattie admitted it was a bore – but the glimpses of an alien way of life. Poor Beattie. Like Mr Ramsbottom from the library with his sea, she'd been avoiding 'socialist' countries for fear of disillusion. She so wanted to approve of East Germany but the best she could manage was a little song of praise for the public transport and wine.

'It's all controlled through the children,' she said of the rest. 'One wrong move, one indiscreet word, and it's your children who'll suffer.'

'How so?' said Andrew.

We'd finished off the travelogue at dinner and were now in the living room drinking coffee and the sloe gin I brew every year from the squire's bushes. I always managed to have some ready for Beattie's visits – it was the only bit of rural life that interested her.

'The best schools, the university places, the choice of which subject to study, the good jobs: if you want your children to have all that, you behave yourself.'

'I see,' said Andrew. He didn't sound too displeased. Years of teaching at a public school had tarnished his liberal views. Also, he was always having to defend himself against Mike, who taught in a comprehensive. At some point defence turned offence. Hence his suspicion of Beattie.

'Infertility must be a great relief,' I said. I was, of course, thinking of my own ravenous womb and the difficulties I was having keeping it in check.

'Hardly. People who don't have children are invisible.' She noticed Andrew's smirk. 'I don't know what you're so pleased about,' she said. 'It's no different here.'

'Hear, hear,' I echoed, but it was probably only the sloe gin. I got up and refilled the glasses.

'Balls,' said Andrew. 'Look at Heath and he doesn't have kids.'

I should point out that however tarnished his liberalism, Andrew never went so far as to become a Tory.

'Look at you two,' Beattie countered, 'trying not to have children and having to fight the state.'

'My doctor isn't the state,' I said. 'Anyway, it's our own fault. We're just mean. You can get vasectomies, you just have to pay extra and have it done privately.'

'Exactly. Privately. The state does not permit. How much is it anyway?'

'Forty quid,' I said.

'I'll give it to you for Christmas.'

I laughed, then saw Andrew's face. 'That's not the point,' I said. 'We could afford it. It's the principle of the thing.'

'Your body is not a principle,' said Beattie.

Nor a radiator. I was beginning to wonder what it was. Increasingly it seemed to be a battleground. Like my garden. How to oppose the life-force run wild. I weed my garden. So does my mother, though it doesn't occur to her that weeds too possess life.

'Hollyhock,' said Beattie, and I knew she was in earnest. Hollyhock was my father's pet name for me. Beattie only borrowed it when she was feeling parental. 'Hollyhock, I hate to think of you ruining your body for a principle.'

I went into the kitchen and made some more coffee. It was a deliberate move. I knew she wouldn't pursue the subject in my absence and by the time I returned Andrew would have steered the conversation onto something different. The truth was, I had no idea whether Andrew would consider a vasectomy even if it were 'free'. And after years of having to pay for even the Pill, that at least had become 'free', just a few months before. Somehow it was easier to latch onto that, call it a principle, and drop the subject.

I returned too soon.

'But *all* states retain power through children,' Beattie was saying.

'All right, the NHS is behind the times,' said Andrew. 'But it's only one small part of the state.'

'It reflects the whole,' said Beattie.

'Coffee!' I sang out.

They stopped long enough for me to fill the cups and for Beattie to light a cigarette. Then she was off again. 'The primary concern of every government – right or left – is to maintain power. You agree?'

Andrew agreed.

'The best way to maintain power is to maintain stability. You agree?'

Andrew thought about this a moment – he knew it was a trap – but he had to agree.

'What is the oldest, the most fundamental, symbol of stability? The family. The Royal Family, the nuclear family, the extended family of the commune – any family, as long as it has children in it to make quite sure the parents don't get up to anything.'

'Political paranoia.'

'Not at all. I don't believe in conspiracy theories. There doesn't have to be a conspiracy – because most people *want* stability.'

I agreed. 'I'd like a little stability.'

She turned on me. 'Holly, I despair of you. You're such a political *naïve*. You're so passive.'

'So what's wrong with stability?' said Andrew.

She turned on Andrew. 'Fine, if you're one of the haves.'

He groaned.

'Yes, "here she goes again". But the have-nots won't disappear just because you groan. They won't disappear until enough people stop turning inward to their children and start looking out at what's going on in the world and questioning the status quo.'

'Which you do,' said Andrew.

'Yes, and which I attempt to teach my students to do.'

'You haven't exactly changed the world,' he said.

'No, and I won't, as long as it's full of bird-brains like Holly –'

Andrew laughed.

'– and fat self-satisfied public schoolteachers like you.'

Andrew stopped laughing.

'Camille's doing something to change the world,' I volunteered. I'd been keeping quiet, waiting for a chance to change the subject.

'What?' Beattie asked.

'She's starting some kind of ginger group to agitate for more free nurseries.'

As soon as I said it I wished I hadn't. Both Andrew and Beattie laughed.

'You see?' said Beattie. 'The minute she has children all she can think about is providing for them.'

'What's wrong with that?' said Andrew.

'Nothing. She's absolutely right. Those children are now her main responsibility in life. She's no longer free to look beyond them. It would be wrong of her to do anything that damaged their future. Just like in the DDR.'

Full circle. I poured out some more sloe gin, though heaven knows none of us needed it.

'Choice, Holly.' (Why she directed this at me when I had already chosen I don't know.) 'I have nothing against children. But you can't be a parent *and* a radical. They cancel each other out. You have to choose.'

I laughed. 'I have chosen. But I'm hardly a radical.'

'True. You're a great disappointment to me.' But she smiled as she said it.

17

Paint my garden lilac. They come in every colour now, and in big fat doubles, too. But my predecessors either didn't know, couldn't find, or didn't want these new-fangled things. Thus: a modest group of modest *Syringa vulgaris* – plain, single, lilac-coloured lilacs. The scent isn't modest, though; great waves of it march along the curved paths, filling all but a few stingy corners with their perfume. The house is perfumed, too. This isn't the time of year for jars to sit empty gathering dust. Every room has its quota of bushy branches, and the open windows become genial battlegrounds for indoor and outdoor variations.

I was sitting by the lilacs when I saw the deer. A twig broke in the squire's wood and I looked up to see a young roe stag. He didn't see me, and no doubt the scent of lilac masked my own scent of wonder. Who wouldn't wonder? What sight more beautiful than a brand new stag lusty with life? I later deduced it was a yearling freshly expelled from Eden by his parents and searching for a territory of his own. He took a few steps and stopped by a young oak I'd planted out several years before. I hardly noticed the tree; I was busy trying to memorize all that beauty, press it hard into my brain cells for future recollection when I needed a little pick-up. The setting sun was behind him, making him glow a soft reddish brown against the equally soft green of early summer. Then he lowered his exquisite head, placed his antlers in the centre of the sapling, and began moving them back and forth. The motion accelerated, slowly at first, then faster, and soon I could see nothing but a reddish green blur as the antlers furiously whipped the branches of my helpless oak into shreds.

18

Once the routine of daily life was established, it went on
much the same for several years. The only significant event
was the birth of Camille's second child. The new one was
a boy, Dominic. He was a much nicer baby than Emma, so
quiet that apart from the extra nappies and feedings it made
little difference to me that my Emma-days had turned into
Emma-and-Dominic days. In fact, so quiet was he that
Camille feared he was subnormal and took him the round
of doctors for reassurance that he was simply a nice baby.

Few people remember that for us in the north 1975 was
a drought year nearly as earnest as the more famous one
that followed. My garden didn't do badly. I always soak
young trees and shrubs in the spring and then mulch them
with compost. Most of the older perennials had long enough
roots to fend for themselves. That left only the newer ones
and the annuals and Andrew's vegetable patch. When the
hosepipe ban came, Mike and Andrew diverted the bathtub
drain into a barrel by the house. It was a drag watering
everything by hand but we managed, and on the day of our
family gathering the garden was looking quite splendid.

It wasn't an official occasion. Mummy and Daddy just
happened to be staying at Ryegill the same time Andrew's
parents were staying with us. When Gillian *et al.* stopped
yet again *en route* to or from Scotland, someone did a little
head-counting and counted enough for a get-together.

There was no question of having it at Ryegill. Camille

couldn't cope with all those people and Andrew's parents couldn't cope with Ryegill. Gillian & Co. had to stay there because we were full up, and they were barely coping either. Ryegill was one of those places with a permanent air of being about-to-be-done-up. The basics were there but not much else.

So I volunteered. I didn't mind. It was the time of year when there's not a lot to do in the garden, and I'd had the previous day (Saturday) off to do most of the cooking in advance. To tell you the truth, I was looking forward to a chance to show off the garden. Obviously we couldn't eat in the house (there were fourteen heads), so what could be more natural than a leisurely buffet on the patio? Then someone pointed out that strolling through the garden with plate in hand was not on when four of the heads were children's, so we changed it to a sit-down lunch. We borrowed extra tables and chairs and made a kind of High Table on the patio instead.

In a way, there were fifteen heads. Barnaby had turned up that morning to rehang some slates broken loose by a freak gale a few weeks before. When he saw bits of family drift in, he tried to drift off, so I took his ladder away. Barnaby, trapped on the roof, glared down at me.

'We can't let you go,' I said. 'What happens if there's another gale what with all those slates flapping around already?'

I was appealing to his professional pride. It worked. He carried on, though with a face gone darkly ominous. The damaged slates were at the front of the house and the patio was at the back, so I didn't see it would make much difference to anyone, but Andrew's mother didn't approve.

'Why does he have to do it on a Sunday?'

'He's in demand,' I said. 'When he gets behind he sometimes works weekends to catch up. We're very lucky to have him at all.'

She frowned and I realized she was thinking of the overtime. Like most rich people, Andrew's parents are mean.

'He doesn't charge overtime,' I added.

The company had assembled. Andrew was playing bartender while I finished setting the table. It really did look lovely. I'd got hold of an immensely long dazzling white tablecloth. So dazzling was it that you hardly noticed the peculiar miscellany of crockery and cutlery borrowed from friends. The best part was the flowers: bowls and bowls of sweet peas scattered artlessly about. Sweet peas aren't easy up here (the short season as well as the gales) and I was terribly proud of these, though really I'd just hit on a good year.

I leaned over one bowl for a long luxurious sniff. When I straightened up, our guests were gone, swallowed up by the garden. They were, as I'd hoped, wandering around the secretive paths, drinks in hand, admiring ... shall we say ... nature?

I don't take as much credit for the garden as may seem. Much of the work was done by my predecessors, and much of the work now is done by, yes, nature – the plants themselves. This is the glory of plants: you give them a little help and they do the rest themselves. I'm merely a partner, a caretaker even. So when I came around the first bend and saw my parents-in-law admiring a sassy little clump of cornflowers, I felt pleased on behalf of the cornflowers. And the cornflowers felt pleased with themselves, or so it seemed. Sometimes I think the plants in my garden preen for visitors; flowers turn their faces to admirers, branches flick their limpid wrists in false modesty. It amuses me to see them show off. I do nothing to curb their vanity. I watched as Mummy took my mother-in-law and Gillian aside and pointed out a rose in the hedge. It was a Mme Isaac Pereire and Mummy was explaining its history. Her language was more florid than the rose itself, but I didn't mind and neither did the rose, which lifted a huge crimson cup in an irresistible invitation to sniff. Most of the men had gone to Andrew's vegetable patch, along with ever-practical Camille and most of the children.

We were in no hurry to eat. I'd deliberately planned a cold lunch to accommodate for lingering. It was a beautiful hot day; not much bird song (they were recovering after their own early lunch) but what there was was deliciously soporific, a taunting contrast to the holiday-makers' cars whizzing unseen past the front of the house. I went to the front and called up to Barnaby and asked him to join us. He replied that he'd already eaten, which was probably true; though flexible about working days, he stuck rigorously to his workman's stomach which dictated 12.00 a.m. But he wouldn't have come if he'd been starving. He'd taken one look at my mother-in-law and summed her up; she belonged the other side of the stile, on the squire's estate, not here with me or Camille or Barnaby. I returned his ladder as a gesture of good will.

The lunch went very well, apart from a few ecological jibes from Camille. I'd taken care to cook some of the children's favourites, less out of love than a desire for peace. I'd also calculated that with four parents and four grandparents, the ratio was just about right. All eight vied for the children's attention, swamping them and leaving little space for anarchy. Seeing us all that day you would have thought us the perfect family. Well, perhaps we were.

I should have anticipated the photograph. We were all so pretty in our pristine summer clothes . . . 'pretty as a picture' said Mummy . . . and that was that.

But who was to take it?

'Get that young workman to come down,' said my mother-in-law.

I cringed. Either Barnaby was one of us or he wasn't. Andrew looked uneasy too, but in the end he went around the front and called down Barnaby.

It took a long time to compose the photograph. I watched Barnaby all the while. Barnaby is tall and thin with a tall thin face that looks as if it's been squashed from the sides, marooning all his features in the middle. He has long almost-black hair and a mephistophelean moustache and goatee. In other circumstances he can appear striking, though not exactly what you'd call handsome, but in his boiler suit he looks like a yobbo. Only when he opens his mouth do people find out he's not.

He wasn't opening his mouth that day. He stood there patiently while various cameras were passed to him and explained by their anxious owners. He waited for the signal. Click. Click. Click. Then back to his rooftop eyrie. I wonder if anyone else saw the sardonic little bow he made just before leaving.

Everything went wrong after that. When we returned to our half-eaten desserts the mood had somehow altered. The festive inanities that knit together disparate families no longer seemed possible and we had nothing in common to take their place. The only sound was the tap tap of Barnaby's hammer or whatever it was he used and the slurp of children enjoying their desserts.

Then I saw Gillian's face. It was wearing a Mona Lisa smirk I should have recognized but didn't – the time lapse had been too long. I don't know if she meant to reveal it then. She may just have thrown it out to break the silence. It did that.

'This seems an appropriate moment to make an announcement,' she said. 'Des and I are expecting another baby.'

There was a different kind of silence, then a flurry of congratulations which in my memory takes on a high excited pitch. Into it a lower note is sounded. Camille: 'Haven't you heard of the population explosion?'

The silence changed quality again and I flashed a much too late warning to my obstreperous sister. She'd drunk a lot of wine but it wouldn't have mattered if she hadn't. I recognized her put-your-fists-up-you're-in-for-it-now look from our childhood. Perhaps there was still time? No one could answer her rhetorical question, so I took advantage of the lull:

'Anyone for more raspberry cream? Fresh from Andrew's garden! It'll only go to waste . . .'

Andrew stared first at me and then at Camille. 'Haven't you?' he said to the latter.

'I beg your pardon?' said Camille.

'You've added two yourself.'

'Two is replacement level,' said Camille. It sounded like a recitation from a book.

'Exactly,' said Andrew. 'The status quo. You're defending the status quo.'

Any other time it would have amused me to hear Andrew echoing Beattie's views, but things were getting bad. Our respective parents were shovelling in dessert as if trying to pulverize Camille's words.

'You've spent half this lunch predicting the imminent destruction of the planet through overpopulation as if your kids are miraculously exempt.'

'They are,' said Camille. 'They're not adding to the population, just replacing us when we're gone.'

Andrew rolled his eyeballs theatrically. 'That's what I just said. Look, if we're overpopulated now, as you keep saying we are, we'll be overpopulated for ever as long as people like you keep replacing your-selves.'

Des cleared his throat. 'He does have a point. Mathematically speaking, that is. That is to say, logically, the only way to achieve a lower population is for a substantial number of people to refrain altogether—'

'Look who's talking!'

'At least he's not a hypocrite!' said Gillian. '*He's* not the one who's been going on about overpopulation! If *you* care, *you* do something! We never pretended to care! Why should we? We want children and that's that!'

I admired her in a way – at least she was being honest – but Camille was horrified.

'Jesus!'

This upset Mummy. 'Camille, I don't care how old you are, I won't have you taking the Lord's name in vain.'

Someone snickered, but for once I was grateful to Mummy. The two families were in danger of unravelling and the only way to avoid it was for each to discipline its own.

Gillian didn't see this. She sailed right across the battle-line: 'Anyway,' she said, with a smile which I now think was sadistic, 'we're only making up for Holly not having any.'

'ME?' I looked at Andrew, but nobody else did. Everyone was looking at me. Even Andrew was looking at me.

There was nothing odd about Barnaby inspecting the chimney that day. The fireplace had smoked the last time we'd used it, so naturally we asked Barnaby to check it while he was up there. He looked like a scarecrow, leaning over the chimney and peering in, all arms and legs precariously attached to his beanpole body. Or beanstalk. For a moment his limbs encased in the green boiler suit became tendrils seeking a hold in the chimney's mortar. The Green Man. Mondamin. Tom Bombadil. (Tolkien was in.)

I wasn't paying much attention. I was smarting from the psychic blow delivered over dessert. I'd tried to ignore it at the time, busying myself clearing the table and moving stuff out of the way so there'd be room to arrange the chairs more informally on the patio for coffee. It was probably symbolic that I pushed my own chair right to the edge, a little bit apart from everyone else. Certainly I felt like an outsider.

Sara had disappeared into the garden, followed at a respectful distance by Emma. They were being awfully quiet so I knew they were damaging something, but I didn't care — the bruise on my psyche was cutting out other sensations. Nicholas, Gillian's soon-to-be-superseded youngest, was flinging my heap of gardening sand over the patio in an ill-concealed fit of premature jealousy. Docile Dominic was asleep on his grandmother's lap. Everyone was talking about the children — the usual exchange of anecdotes which parents find amusing. Normally Andrew detested such anecdotes, but today he was laughing as much as the others. Every so often someone shot a meaningful glance in my direction. I answered it with an automatic smile.

The upper half of Barnaby disappeared into the chimney. He was there quite a while. I had visions of him disappearing and re-emerging next December as Father Christmas. From where I was sitting I was the only one who could see him and this seemed to form an invisible line of communication between us, compensation for my new alienation from the family scene on the patio.

Andrew had done it deliberately. I could see that now, and that's why I was smarting. He'd deliberately pushed the onus of not producing children onto me. Why hadn't I said the obvious: 'It takes two, you know'? After all, it was he who was so sure he didn't want children, though I admit that I'd acquiesced readily enough (no doubt aided by the Mrs Potter episode when I was four). What's more, he'd been outspoken in his views. Both sides of the family knew what he thought about children. It was Andrew who complained most about the juvenile takeover of our house

73

and our lives, Andrew who glared at the torrent of children that crammed the trains and buses with their free or cut-price tickets, Andrew who noticed how children and pregnant women were the only ones singled out in casualty figures whenever there was an accident or an I R A bombing.

Barnaby's upper half cranked itself out of the chimney. He was holding something. I squinted to see what it was. Barnaby noticed and tilted the object towards me. It was a nest: slovenly, sooty, and no doubt damaged by its ascent from the chimney. In it I could just about see the corpses of several young birds, probably starlings. I nodded vaguely and Barnaby set the nest on the ridge tiles. I wondered why he didn't put it on the little platform that straddled the ridge and held all his tools but of course that was why – it was full of tools.

If only I'd said, 'It takes two, you know.' Why didn't I? Because unlike Beattie I did not enjoy dissent. Anyway, I was the hostess. Hostesses don't encourage dissent among their guests. Not that that would have stopped Camille. If we'd been at Ryegill she still would have said, 'Haven't you heard of the population explosion?' If we'd been in London Gillian still would have said, 'We're only making up for Holly not having any.' Beattie was right; I was passive. Camille was right, too; I was a flabby bourgeois prig.

Barnaby had finished the roof. I watched him detach the little platform and disappear with it down the catladder on the other side of the roof. Then the end of the catladder wiggled, unhooked itself, and also disappeared. I wondered if I should go around and pay him. We always paid him on the spot and in cash – Barnaby was a hidden economy worth supporting. Then I noticed the nest, still perched on the ridge. Perhaps Barnaby hadn't finished after all.

Another anecdote finished to a round of laughter. I received the meaningful glances with a face gone stony. I was fuming by then. Holly the perfect hostess was imagining herself standing up and interrupting the next anecdote with 'It takes two, you know.' She was watching, in her imagination, the horrified reaction.

She was also watching the bird nest. With the little platform gone, it was open to the light breeze that teased one side of it. It quivered a bit and was still. How very odd of Barnaby to leave it. Barnaby is the most thorough builder in the world. To give but one example: knowing that he would be looking in the chimney today, he'd told me to tape up the fireplace in case any soot came down. How many builders would think of that? No wonder he's in demand.

The gate squeaked and the prostrate houseladder slid to rest against the side of the house. A moment later I heard the cough of Barnaby's van starting up. I started up, too. I'm not sure what I meant to do: rush around to pay him or remind him about the bird nest or deliver the sentence that was now branded in my mind, but it was as if the motion of Barnaby's van and of my getting up agitated the breeze beyond patience and I saw the nest tilt and then slide slowly down the roof. It paused at the eaves and I swear there was no way Barnaby could have known who was sitting where but the nest and its cargo teetered and then fell off in a sooty arc and came to rest in my mother-in-law's lap just as I stood up and said in a loud clear voice, 'IT TAKES TWO, YOU KNOW.'

19

The following summer Alice moved in next door. She'd spent the intervening six years in communes, all of them as squalid as the one she'd left in California. ('Us guys' evidently don't do these things better over here.) She'd enjoyed the experience though, and was thinking of writing a comparative study of British and American communes – she had a degree in sociology.

Alice didn't come alone. At one of the communes she'd met a girl called Diana. They'd fallen passionately in love and decided they didn't much care for communal body-sharing so they set up house together much as any other starry-eyed couple.

I was delighted with my new neighbours. Detached from her plant-eating son, Alice was the most considerate of people and as sensitive to others as she'd been obtuse before. Diana was harder to know. She'd been a lesbian since her early teens and had suffered from the unpermissive society, but with merry Alice mediating, her wariness subsided. She was short and dumpy like Alice, with an equally round face, but her cropped blonde hair hardened her features while Alice's ginger frizz made a halo not entirely out of keeping with her nature.

I had a vested interest in welcoming them. The people who'd lived there before, a young lorry driver and his wife, had started out as starry-eyed as Alice and Diana, but when the children arrived, and with them the rows, things went downhill pretty fast. Earplugs solved the problem of sleeping through their fights, but there was nothing I could do when the wife left her children with me 'for five minutes while I nip down the road for a loaf of bread' and then sped off for several hours of freedom. I was learning to cope with Emma and Dominic, but four tipped the balance.

Enter Alice and Diana. Not only did they not have children, they helped me with Camille's. Alice had a way with children (she was, after all, an ex-mother) and was happy to distract my charges while I got on with the garden. In fact, my memories of that second drought summer are almost as arcadian as those of Ryegill in its early years. I picture Alice transformed by a rope between her teeth into Ginger the Horse being galloped along the paths by her relentless owner Dominic. Or playing hide and seek in a garden which must have seemed as vast to the children as the squire's estate was to me.

Or Diana, solemnly explaining to Emma why it was not cruel to pinch out the broad bean tops. Diana was into self-sufficiency and working hard to turn their strip of land into a miniature Ryegill. Sometimes we spent the day next door. I'd never been inside the house (the previous woman was of the keep-herself-to-herself variety except when dumping her kids) but had guessed correctly that it was the mirror image of our own. Apart from some evidence of dinners used as missiles, the place was in fairly good nick and needed only a few repairs (by Barnaby – who else?) to make it cosy. They rented, of course – it was still impossible in our town for two women to get a joint mortgage, and they didn't earn all that much anyway.

That was the year Andrew and I went to Italy the second time. His summer job had collapsed with the recession (though it wasn't yet called that), leaving him restless and irritable. I prescribed a holiday and made all the arrangements and off we went.

It wasn't as good as the first one. I'd learned a little Italian by then and had some ideas about what I wanted to see. Andrew trailed along passively and on one occasion made me talk myself out of a mess in Italian, feigning ignorance of the language himself. Perhaps he was just playing the schoolteacher, throwing his pupil in at the deep end, but that doesn't explain why he made me choose where we ate and stayed this time. (Some of my decisions were pretty lousy, too.)

And always the packs of children running wild like dogs and always the old women in black saying, '*Bambini non ci sono? Bambini non ci sono?*'

We returned to find Alice and Diana broke and looking for jobs. That is to say, Alice was looking for a job. Diana had already found one – kitchen assistant at a school – but it didn't start till September. Alice was having more trouble. Jobs were tight even then, and, as usual, the reaction was to exclude foreigners, a reaction made easier by the nuisance of getting a work permit and proving that the foreigner possessed attributes lacking in the natives. Boiling cabbage did not require an American sociology graduate.

Then one of my staff left to have a baby. She didn't intend to return. The job was advertised.

My cousin was very tactful. She said nothing for some time. Then she asked, with a delicacy I appreciated, whether it would cause any embarrassment to me if she applied. I thought about it a moment. No, I said, it wouldn't. She applied.

Mr McDonald had long since moved south and I was now in charge. Normally the County Librarian gave me the final say in new appointments, but on this occasion, with its overtones of nepotism, I didn't want the responsibility. I explained why and she agreed.

As it happened, there was little choice anyway. Most of the applicants were school-leavers or young marrieds. For virtually the same price we could have a graduate with extensive experience of libraries, albeit from a user's point of view. We would also have an American. Americans were still considered second only to Germans as efficient hard workers.

There was an additional factor which I hesitate to mention: mothers are expensive employees. Not only do they get maternity leave, they also absent themselves every time one of the children is ill and then again when they catch these illnesses from their children. All this adds up to a lot of sick leave and a lot of extra work for the rest of the staff. It is, I suspect, one reason women are often paid less: they work less, at least when they're mothers, and all women under forty are potential mothers. Hence, Alice. She'd been a mother once and showed no sign of wishing to repeat the experiment. I don't know if the County Librarian knew Alice was a lesbian. If so, she may well have thought: so much the better. Lesbians don't usually become mothers. My County Librarian and myself are hard-headed professionals. Our job is to give the best service we can.

Hence Alice.

Alice certainly justified our decision. She worked like hell, she was consistently cheerful, and she monitored the Children's Room in a way that minimized the damage without offending youthful egos. She also volunteered for the tasks everyone else hated. One of these was shelving light romances. This can be tricky when a crowd of addicts has gathered in front of sparse shelves. The assistant who goes out with an armload of replenishments is likely to be mobbed, and a few have suffered cuts and bruises in the process. Not Alice. Like a soprano embarking on a strenuous aria, she would plant her feet wide apart while a flurry of hands snatched at her books. A moment later it was over, leaving Alice undamaged, still smiling, and empty-armed. 'That way I don't have to shelve them,' she said. (You see? Efficient.) She didn't even mind. She was now thinking of writing a comparative study of drug and light romance addiction.

It's hardly surprising, then, that the rest of my staff adored her. Most of the borrowers did, too. Even those whose daughters had failed to get her job were reconciled in the end, and the mutters of nepotism ceased. In fact, the whole town took to Alice.

The only person who didn't like Alice was Andrew. He didn't like Diana either. He didn't exactly tell me to stop seeing them, but he hinted that a little less discourse between the two houses would be a good thing.

And yes, there was discourse. I won't deny that Alice and Diana took a dim view of marriage in general and mine in particular. Diana even called Andrew a male chauvinist pig, though not to his face. The awful thing was, I couldn't deny it, at least not as vigorously as I would have liked. In the ten years of our marriage Andrew had changed so gradually I'd hardly noticed. I was noticing now. I'd begun noticing the day of the family get-together when he dumped the onus of childlessness onto me. And now, picturing our marriage through the eyes of Alice and Diana, I was noticing more and more. All this noticing was adding up to something. What it added up to was that Andrew wanted children.

20

Leave my garden bare, a blank white sheet against which the mock orange disappears. When we first came here there was only one, but its fragrant white froth seduced me with visions of procreation. I took cuttings. Now the off-spring surround their parent in a great white mound every June.

I'm a fickle gardener. In lilac time I favour its rich heavy scent. When the mock orange takes over as my garden's centrepiece, I welcome the sharp overtones that balance its sweetness. And when the roses—

But that's another day. I've procrastinated long enough. Let me try now, while my head is filled with the sweet-sharp smell of weddings, to trace the disintegration from my own. This isn't easy. The simple fact is, I have no idea when or how or why Andrew changed. There was no gradual growing awareness, nor was there a single day when suddenly I realized. There was only a time when he didn't want children and then, many years later, a time when he did. And when finally I noticed, even the noticing was vague and timeless and wholly without markers or meaning, so any account I give is bound to be false. The best I can do is gather together and sum up some of the arguments I received piecemeal:

He only disliked other people's children; our own would be different.

He hadn't meant no children for ever; he'd only wanted

a very long time, longer than most, in which to enjoy being married before settling into parenthood.

Why miss out on the experience of having children?

Who would look after us when we were old? (Chilling thought, this; it worked both ways: who would be looking after our parents? The thought of Mummy and me cooped up together made me shiver.)

I countered with arguments he himself had given in what now seemed like a previous existence. (For example, why miss out on the experience of *not* having children?) But he recognized his old words in my mouth and only grew irritable, so I stopped arguing and waited. And while I waited, I thought.

And somewhere along the line a new picture of Andrew emerged. I didn't recognize him. The liberal veneer had finally worn bare to reveal his family: generations of conventional minor gentry who had now reclaimed their own. The real reason Andrew now wanted children was simply that everyone else had them. In addition, he saw his manhood threatened by '*Bambini non ci sono? Bambini non ci sono?*' and by the raised eyebrows of his colleagues. Alice and Diana personified this threat in its worst – i.e. female – form. I shouldn't have been surprised when, in the course of one argument, he referred to my new friends as 'dykes'. The word had never been used in our house. I could almost feel the walls cringe.

Much later, when it was all over, Beattie came up with another explanation, the one I referred to earlier: that I had become too strong for Andrew and the only way he could keep me in my place was to tie me down with children. I don't know what she meant, unless he interpreted my quiet passivity as strength. I sure as hell didn't feel strong. I felt utterly miserable. It had cost Andrew a lot to eat years' worth of words about not wanting children; there was no way he could recant a second time without losing face.

There was also no way I could agree to having children. I simply didn't like them and wasn't convinced that 'our own will be different'.

So there we were. Stalemate. Neither of us could move, and without moving, we couldn't go on together. Something had to happen.

In 1978 Andrew moved in with a peripatetic oboist. She taught one day a week at Andrew's school and had a large flat near the town centre. It was an odd affair, with little passion on either side. Andrew as much as said he was willing to come back to me at any time, but only on one condition.

'You're only thirty-five,' he said on one of his many trips home to collect some suspiciously insignificant item he'd left behind. 'There's still time.'

Five fertile years before the door shut on an invisible woman. I viewed the magic span with resentment.

'No.'

On another visit he accused me of being a careerist. This wasn't true and he knew it. I had no desire to replace the County Librarian. I wanted nothing more than my present job, my garden, and, yes, Andrew.

No deal.

Another time he accused me of being frigid. This was even more untrue and a bit much coming from someone whose interest in sex had declined in inverse proportion to his desire for children.

'Go back to your oboist,' I said. (He'd come back for pyjamas that day so I was feeling a little smug.)

Was my consciousness being raised by the lesbian citadel next door? Indeed it was. None the less, I continued to defend Andrew. God knows why. Such are the habits of marriage.

A few months later the headship of the classics department of a prestigious public school near London was advertised. He who had accused me of rampant careerism applied and was appointed. He who detested other people's children moved in with Des, Gillian and their brood of four – just temporarily, of course; he was looking for a house for 'us'. Evidently it wasn't temporary enough, for a few months later Des moved out. Nobody seemed to notice.

By now my consciousness had been raised to somewhere in the stratosphere. Everywhere I looked I saw the pressures being put on women to breed and the subtle (and sometimes not so subtle) discrimination against those who refused. I also saw that we had far more in common with lesbians and even with male homosexuals than we did with heterosexuals who had children. We were all of us outsiders, and outsiders who (as Beattie had said) threatened the stability of the state.

Paranoia? Perhaps, or so I kept telling myself. All this consciousness raising wasn't helping me one little bit. I still missed Andrew. I wonder even now if I would have welcomed back a repentant Andrew. I'm not so sure. Passionless or not, his affair had hurt me far more than he realized.

Alice was surprisingly sympathetic. She'd never been as militant as Diana and seemed to understand that love and sex and jealousy are disrespectful of gender. She looked at the large, ageing, stodgy abandoned librarian and saw not a case for conversion but a wounded human. I was very grateful and in the years following came to love my funny American cousin. I even considered becoming a lesbian but I wasn't sure how one went about it. I remember one evening when the three of us were sitting around my kitchen table and I looked at Alice and tried to imagine making love with her. I tried quite hard but it just didn't seem to work. Many years later Alice reminded me of that evening. She and Diana had known what I was thinking. They were relieved I didn't try harder. In the end, so was I, for Barnaby was about to change my life.

21

Barnaby and I first met when we were students. He lived
in Beattie's house, one of those immensely tall thin Victorian
terraces that form the main residential areas of most redbrick
universities. This one had five storeys, if you counted the
half-basement and the attic. Obviously one person couldn't
possibly use all that space, so she turned several rooms into
bedsits which she let at a modest rent to refugees from the
halls of residence. There were two conditions: the lodgers
must not be from her own department; and they must agree
in writing to a list of rules, nearly all of which concerned
noise. The rules were off-putting to the average student.
There was, none the less, a long waiting list for her rooms.
She required no references. Instead, she interviewed the
applicant. Only once did she make a wrong decision; the
rest of her lodgers stayed on till they left university.

Barnaby had the attic – he was so sensitive to noise that
even footsteps disturbed him. I never saw his attic. In fact,
I didn't meet Barnaby till he'd lived there nearly three
years. Camille and I seldom visited Beattie – partly because
she didn't encourage visitors but also because we were wary
of relatives in this our first freedom from Family.

In the spring of 1964 Beattie held a party. She did this
every year as a kind of letting-go before exams. Not that
her parties were relaxing. There was no music or dancing
and only the basics in food (bread, cheese, salami, crisps,
celery). There was, however, an abundance of booze, the

idea being to loosen tongues for talk. That it certainly did. The guests included other lecturers, graduate students, a few favoured undergraduates, all the lodgers, and, in 1964, her nieces. We were pretty awed by the assemblage and spent the first hour tanking up and talking to each other as if we were long lost friends instead of sisters who saw each other practically every day. Then I saw Barnaby.

Love at first sight? Hardly. He was very nearly ugly and in his black beatnik garb made a gloomy accent point in the décor of Beattie's party. I think I felt sorry for him. He was all by himself with not even a sister to share his awkwardness. I introduced myself, followed closely by Camille, and made the brilliant opening, 'What are you studying?'

'Architecture.'

'How fascinating.'

'Yes.'

'What kinds of things do you want to design?'

'Council houses.'

'How interesting.'

The conversation might have died there if Camille hadn't stepped in. She *was* interested, and soon they were discussing the role of politics in town planning. Barnaby was slightly ahead of his time. While admiring the Bauhaus initiative, he was upset by its debasement into the high-rises it had spawned. If an Englishman's home was his castle – an idea he deplored but realistically accepted – then every Englishman should have one and not be fobbed off with a little cube within a big cube. What did he have in mind, I asked. Individual houses, he said, which would be cheap enough to win a council tender but not be an insult to their inhabitants. The problem, he went on, was that houses that were cheap to build were usually expensive to run. This created hardship, then resentment, and, finally, dereliction of the property. He was looking for a compromise that wasn't a compromise.

'How interesting,' I repeated. A graduate student I knew from the English Department had just come in. I made my excuses and left Barnaby to Camille.

I didn't see him again for over two years and completely forgot he existed. Meanwhile, Andrew and I had met, married, and moved north. One Saturday morning we were in the ironmonger's buying a curtain rail for our flat above the butcher's. The tall skinny man ahead of us in the queue turned around. It was Barnaby. I recognized him immediately, despite the boiler suit that had replaced his black sweater and jeans. I even remembered his name. (He didn't remember mine.) I was so tickled to see an old face in a new place that I greeted him with more enthusiasm than the occasion warranted. It was not reciprocated. One of Barnaby's clients wanted a particular kind of door fitment his supplier didn't have, so he was having to buy it here at the retail price. This offended his professional pride and made him grumpy. Andrew (who at that time was still liberal and thus approved of the working class) asked him to join us for coffee next door. Barnaby accepted.

'Are you still designing council houses?' I asked when we'd settled ourselves into the café.

He gave me a peculiar look. 'No.' Evidently it was an inadequate reply to someone who'd just bought him a coffee, and he added, 'No time for that. I have to earn a living.'

Gradually, over two coffees and countless pastries, we elicited some kind of life history. Barnaby had been raised in a series of Yorkshire towns which included the one we were sitting in now. His father had been first a builder's labourer, then a builder, and finally the owner of a timber yard. Barnaby had worked with and for his father but had become dissatisfied with the buildings he helped to construct. He went back to school for some A-levels and then on to university. He knew what he wanted to design; what he needed was the technical expertise for putting it on paper plus a qualification which would persuade people to take those designs seriously. This he got. Unfortunately, he hadn't been able to get into an established firm and didn't have the capital to set up by himself, so he'd fallen back on his building skills.

When I expressed sympathy he seemed surprised. He didn't mind at all. With no family to support and no employees (he hired casual help when needed), he could undercut everyone else. In addition, he offered the unique perk of architectural advice at no extra cost. He was doing very nicely. In time he would set up a combined architectural and building firm. Then he'd be able both to design houses and to put some of those designs into practice. He would also be able to select his clients.

'Council houses?' I asked again.

Again the peculiar look. 'No.'

It was Barnaby who found us this house and Barnaby who did most of the difficult work, with Andrew and myself acting as navvies at the weekends. Barnaby liked small houses because they offered more scope for intelligent design. Our central heating, for example. He installed a simple system using a particularly efficient back boiler behind the living room fireplace. In addition, he made sure none of the pipework was buried under concrete or floorboards. It ran along the walls and was neatly boxed in with screw-on panels so that if a leak developed, it could be repaired without ripping the house apart. This was not startlingly revolutionary, just the ordinary intelligent thinking which soon made him the town's most sought-after builder.

The three of us worked well together. Some initial suspicion faded when he discovered that his middle-class 'clients' were willing to muck in and take instructions from him. I remember one day in particular. We were in the living room. Barnaby was installing the back boiler while Andrew and I, miniature pick-axes in hand, hacked the sodden old plaster off the walls. We were all quite filthy: Barnaby with soot and us with powdery plaster fall-out. The room was filthy, too, and I was wondering how it would ever be inhabitable. To divert my apprehensions I asked once again about the council houses Barnaby had evidently abandoned. He looked up at me like a black and white minstrel through his soot, perhaps wondering if we were worthy of his confidence. He took a sounding:

'They're all family-sized jobs,' he said.

'So?' I asked.

Barnaby retreated. 'It's a bad size,' was all he said. 'Small buildings, fine. Big buildings – say, a four-flat block with all the services run centrally from a basement – that's fine too. Anything between you can't do much with.'

'Surely that's a challenge?' said Andrew.

Barnaby busied himself with the fireproof cement. Then he took another sounding:

'Not all challenges are worth it,' he said.

'What does that mean?' said Andrew.

Barnaby carefully cemented in some part of the back boiler. It took a long time. Andrew and I were just about to resume our own work when Barnaby spoke again.

'Look, I'd like to work for a local authority,' he said. 'Soon as they start building for something other than families I'll be right in there, all right? Can you pass me that wrench?'

What Barnaby was trying to say was Small is Beautiful, though the book hadn't been written yet. I suppose you could call him a radical – wanting to build for those who would challenge the status quo – but the word sits oddly on

Barnaby. At any rate, I paid no more attention to him than to Beattie. My main concern was to finish the house and move into it. When we did, Barnaby dropped out of our lives. This was more his fault than ours. We invited him around several times but he always declined. Pressure of work, he said. When he got home in the evening all he could do was flop, he said. He was not being entirely honest. He was, in fact, a loner. Daily contact with clients and suppliers was more than enough for him. At night he valued his solitude.

He resurfaced briefly during the Ryegill period. Then, apart from odd repairs, he disappeared from our lives again. Only when Andrew disappeared from mine did Barnaby make his final entrance.

22

I was in my office that day. I spent a lot of time in my office after Andrew took up with his oboist. Our town is not, as Barnaby claims, an oversize Ambridge, but word does get around and Andrew was hardly discreet, flaunting his floozy in the middle of town. I couldn't bear a whole day's worth of pitying looks from my borrowers. Worse still, as the months went by and Andrew moved to London, some of the looks turned from pity to something like satisfaction. Andrew had told his friends why he'd left me. This naturally aroused the sympathy of many mothers and fathers. Since most towns are composed mainly of mothers and fathers, I was beginning to feel as Andrew no doubt wished me to feel: an obstinate, unreasonable, unnatural woman.

I also felt something he didn't intend: resentment. This had repercussions for my work. Influenced by Alice and Diana and Beattie and perhaps even the absent Barnaby, I was ordering books on ecology, feminism and radical politics. I was cunning, though. With each batch of orders I tucked in just one or two subversives, and those were carefully chosen. There was no point buying serious tomes no one would read, so I went for the popular end of the market.

These were hard times for libraries. Even before Thatcher, finances were diminishing. Already one full-time staff member had gone the way of 'natural wastage' and our book allocation was shrinking like a pork chop in hot fat.

We were urged to make most of our cuts in fiction. This grieved me. In revenge, and in contravention of the first principle of librarianship (what the borrower wants, the borrower gets), I made my cuts at the lower end. My latest atrocity had been to pass over a new Cartland in favour of Joanna Russ's *The Female Man*. I was flicking through the pages (tough but readable – I hoped someone would) when Barnaby knocked and entered.

I'd like to report that he gazed with awe and wonder at a new radicalized Holly resplendent in dungarees and hacked hair and with her feet on the desk. Sadly, this was not so. The reaction to both Andrew's departure and the lesbian camp next door was the opposite extreme; my appearance became respectable to the point of dowdy – in preparation, perhaps, for the invisibility which would overcome me at age forty. Feet on the desk? Never!

I peered at him over my ugly new NHS reading glasses and prepared to greet him warmly.

He gave me no chance. 'I want to order some stuff,' he said.

This was a dumb opening. Barnaby had been ordering 'stuff' for years. He was well acquainted with the pile of request cards on the issue desk; he had used them without prompting before, mainly to order boring tracts on the latest developments in building and architecture. Temporary amnesia was unlikely. Barnaby was up to something.

Like all Englishwomen faced by a man who is up to something, I displayed no reaction. 'What kind of stuff?' I said.

He reached into his boiler suit pocket for a crumpled list. As he handed it over, I felt a perverse surge of affection for his grubby fingernails. I scanned the list. It was straightforward enough; all of it could be borrowed from Boston Spa. I took some order cards from a drawer and invited him to sit down and fill them out. He did so.

I looked at his head bent over the cards. There were grey hairs among the black. This startled me. There were grey hairs among mine, too, but that seemed reasonable. Barnaby wasn't the sort of person who was supposed to grow old.

A member of staff knocked and came in. The van had come to unload but the back room was packed full of books waiting to go onto the mobile which was due to arrive and depart an hour ago. Crisis. (My staff love crises – they liven up the day.) I went to sort it out.

When I returned, Barnaby had finished his cards and was standing by the window. It overlooked a rainsoaked alley. There was nothing to see. Something was definitely up.

'How are you?' I asked.

'Fine.'

'How's business?'

'Pretty good.'

We talked about this a while. He'd taken on an apprentice in the hope of gaining more time for design, but all that happened was the volume of work increased proportionately. If he had a dozen apprentices, the work would increase a dozen-fold. I accused him of ingratitude and raised a small smile.

Alice came in. Some kid had puked over a pile of books; did I have any of those paper thingies soaked in cologne to get rid of the stink? I reached into petty cash and told her to buy some at Boots. She left.

Barnaby was still there.

'So how are you?' he asked.

'Fine.'

I could read on his squashed face that he knew I'd been abandoned. In an ordinary man this would have explained his visit, but Barnaby wasn't ordinary and I wasn't in the mood to discuss my personal life. 'Are you being more selective about your clients these days?' I asked.

Yes, he was.

'Do I still qualify?' A child had torn off a downpipe of my house trying to climb it; I asked if Barnaby would consider repairing it when he had time.

He would.

Another girl came in. Mrs Trevelyan had ordered a biography of some Royal or other months ago and today she just happened to walk past the bookshop and see it displayed in the window. She was sure Mrs Moore had queue-jumped her on the waiting list. (Mrs Moore was her great rival at the Lit. & Phil. Soc.)

I looked in the files. The book was at HQ being processed. It would be here next week. The girl threw me a panicky look. Evidently Mrs Trevelyan counted as a crisis. I went out to add authority to the progress report.

When I returned, Barnaby was still there. He was beginning to get on my nerves. 'Barnaby,' I said, 'I don't want to sound rude, but why exactly are you here?'

'Oh. I thought I might ask you to lunch.'

'Have you had long enough to think about it?'

'Pardon?'

'What's the verdict? Do I get lunch or not?'

We went to the Fox and Hounds. The name indicates its main clientele, but it also has good food and so is frequented by quite a range of people. I've probably given the wrong impression about this town. We do have our squirearchy and retired gentlefolk and the class which Diana calls Sloane Ranger. But there are also smaller farmers, as well as the usual bank clerks and estate agents and solicitors and teachers and preachers. It's true that we have a blacksmith who actually shoes horses, but other shops sell spuds and plastic trinkets. A flourishing launderette indicates that not everybody is rich, though some of the customers use it only to wash horseblankets deemed too dubious for their own machines. Apart from an internationally famous factory that makes fire extinguishers, there is no working class, but a multitude of agricultural service industries provide ample employment.

Any of these people (except perhaps the preachers) are likely to be found in the Fox and Hounds. Even so, we must have looked an odd pair: Barnaby in his boiler suit, me in my ancient twin set (no pearls) and baggy tweed skirt and sensible shoes just a fraction run down at the heel.

There was game pie on the menu. I wondered if that meant rabbits and hares and deer. If so, my teeth would enjoy sinking into the flesh that fed off my garden. Then I remembered the runaway pheasants who scratched their harmless living beneath my shrubs in snowy winters. I asked the girl behind the bar.

She consulted a corner of the ceiling to ascertain the season (September). 'Mostly grouse and hares,' she said.

I weighed up the heroes and villains and ordered lasagne. Barnaby ordered a ploughman's lunch. We both had beer. We eyed each other over our glasses. Away from my lair and the brass plaque proclaiming my importance I was clearly less august. Barnaby came right out with it.

'I hear Andrew has left you.'

I nodded. 'He's also left his oboist. Or hadn't you heard that?'

He hadn't.

'Two weeks ago,' I said. 'Your jungle telegraph's got a fault on the line.'

It was a cute remark out of character. I was making quite a few such remarks these days. Barnaby digested this one along with a lump of cheese and then said, 'How do you feel about it all?'

'Furious.'

He smiled. His smile, unlike many I'd received lately, had no malice in it. It suddenly occurred to me that this luncheon date might be his attempt to provide me with a visible male admirer to counteract Andrew's ladyfriend. I was touched at the thought. I compared our two prizes. Mine was infinitely superior.

'I wanted to see if you were all right,' he said.

Nobody else had said that. Nobody had even alluded to my new status as abandoned wife. That's how I knew they knew.

'I am,' I said. 'I've got quite chummy with the girls next door. We sit around the kitchen at night like Macbeth's witches.'

We talked about that a while. (Alice and Diana were not aggressive lesbians, but they preferred people to know.) Barnaby's reaction was interesting. No mention of 'dykes' and nothing that even Diana could reasonably call male chauvinist. Just curiosity. I'd forgotten his dislike of families and only some way through the conversation realized he was making space to accommodate lesbians in his master-plan to subvert the status quo.

This led me to confide my own master-plan for subverting the library's stock. He seemed amused at the idea of a librarian subverting anything and I had to remind him sharply that designing houses for non-existent child-free people wasn't exactly very useful either. We agreed we were both useless and went on to the next topic.

This was the garden. Barnaby must have been feeling sorry for me to ask after my garden because he wasn't the least bit interested in gardens, my own or anyone else's. Neither was Beattie. It became a source of friction with both of them. They always wanted to know what *use* a garden was if it didn't grow vegetables. To speak of usefulness to a woman with a BA in English is manifestly absurd, and I offered none of the usual excuses. They wouldn't understand that even if no one – even myself – used the garden, it still needed to exist. The thought of my garden living and breathing and doing its thing unseen throughout the night gave me an irrational sense that the universe, as long as it contained my garden, might be salvaged.

But my garden was used. It had been used on the day Andrew turned against me. 'Barnaby,' I said. 'That bird nest. Did you know where it was going to fall?'

'What bird nest?'

I recounted the events of that day in detail. Barnaby remembered everything but the bird nest. I studied his face. A Chinaman's face is a cornucopia of expression compared to Barnaby's. I decided there are some things one just shouldn't ask him.

'Are you doing anything on Sunday?' he said as we emerged from the pub onto the wet street.

'Weeding my useless garden – if it stops raining.'

'Is it urgent?'

'Gardens are always urgent. Do you want to ask me out?' We were approaching the library and with it my august persona. I could feel it radiating out to meet me and to tie poor Barnaby's tongue in knots again.

Then he uttered the two most startling sentences I have ever heard. Even the event which several years later earned me considerable notoriety is nothing compared to the shock value of Barnaby's next words:

'I wondered if maybe you'd like to come to my place. There's something I want to ask you about.'

23

Nobody, it was rumoured, had ever been allowed inside Barnaby's house. This wasn't strictly true but near enough to explain my astonishment at his invitation. Few people even knew where he lived. This was no bad thing, I decided that Sunday when I saw his house. No one seeing that house would ever have hired him.

It was an old vicarage belonging to a remote hill parish which had long since ceased to exist. The church had disappeared along with most of the houses – I don't know why – and the vicarage looked in imminent danger of doing likewise. We approached it from a long and nearly impassable track which jolted the van's innards so badly that I, no lover of machines, felt pity for this one.

The kempt pastures of the estate (not my squire's but another's) stopped abruptly at a decrepit dry stone wall. We drove through a gateless gateway into what presumably had been a traditional vicarage garden, though only a botanical archaeologist could now discern any trace of it. The grass, unmown for decades, had grown into a rank and reedy coverall useless even to the sheep who strayed in and quickly strayed out again.

We walked to the front door past rusted remains of previous vans. I couldn't believe it. Barnaby, the neatest and tidiest and most considerate of builders, lived here?

The house itself was straight out of a gothic novel, one of those rambling places that had been added to and subtracted from so much that to describe it would defeat all but the cleverest writer. I will say only that we passed through a series of rooms each more appalling than the last. Most of the downstairs appeared to be given over to tools and machinery and various building materials. There was also some ancient furniture, left over from its vicarage days and now moulding gently in forgotten corners. The kitchen was unbelievable. No one could possibly eat a meal prepared in it.

The first floor contained bedrooms which had clearly not been used for decades. When I opened the door to one, an inch-thick layer of dust undulated and frowned at the intrusion. There was also a bathroom from which one was unlikely to emerge much cleaner than one entered. I shut the door and followed Barnaby to the top floor.

This was in effect a dormer attic with more bedrooms (servants?) along one side and three closed doors on the other. The middle one was oak, beautifully restored and looking absurdly out of place in its surroundings. Barnaby opened it and gestured me in.

What I walked into was a rural penthouse-cum-studio. The main outside wall had been turned into a continuous dormer window illuminating a long narrow room. On the left was Barnaby's work area with a draughtsman's table, trestle tables, shelves and drawers, anglepoise lamps and mysterious bits and pieces all neatly arranged and purposeful. The oak floor had been as lovingly restored as the door and gleamed, dustless, in the bright north light.

On the right, and differentiated by a large square of extremely clean carpet, was a living area. The furniture was plain but good: a single divan bed with a handwoven spread and several cushions, an immensely inviting easy chair, a bookcase, a chest of drawers, a wardrobe, a small dining table and single ladderback chair.

I suppose Barnaby is such a loner he forgets how others

might view his eccentricities. I had barely taken in the extraordinary room when he said, in his flat voice, 'Tea?'

I nodded and took up the easy chair's invitation. Barnaby went to a tiny built-in kitchen unit and filled the kettle. Questions were piling up in my mind. While the tea brewed, I began.

'How did you get planning permission?'

'I didn't.'

'Aren't you risking your position?'

He shrugged.

We drank our tea and I interrogated him. He seemed to expect it, so perhaps he wasn't as ignorant of his image as I thought. The house, he explained, had been very cheap. It was too big for a family house (I smiled at this but he didn't notice), too remote for a nursing home, too poorly situated for a country hotel. He had simply waited as the price went down and then bought. Since a grant would have meant doing up the whole house, he did without. Yes, he thought the long dormer window wouldn't have got planning permission. Who was there to tell?

I got up and looked out of the window. It was at the back of the house. Outside, a scattering of mute sheep grazed a not too distant moor. Barnaby's sleek and silent countryside before The Fall. It occurred to me that this was his garden. Then I remembered the actual garden in front, and the rambling house beneath us.

'If you're so worried about population,' I said, 'why are you taking up all this space yourself?'

'Yes, well . . .' He poured out more tea. There was a proper sugar bowl and milk jug and a plate of biscuits. Barnaby just didn't add up. 'Any suggestions?' he said.

'Me?'

'Well, I thought about turning it into flats for single people, but people who like this kind of country don't want to be stuck with a lot of other people, do you think?'

'Is this what you wanted to ask me?'

'Not exactly. Well, part of it, maybe. But it's not important. I reckon to be here a long time yet.'

I felt oddly reassured. That Barnaby should continue to exist in his bizarre eyrie was suddenly as important as my garden's role in keeping the universe together.

My garden reminded me of the plant, an enormous grape ivy I'd noticed in one corner of Barnaby's work area. I got up again and went to have a closer look. It seemed in excellent health. 'You obviously don't need my advice on this,' I said.

He got up and joined me. 'No. It's this,' he said. He pointed to one of the trestle tables. On it were models of houses, tiny models of tiny houses. It took me some time to decipher what was going on in them. There was no furniture or decoration but a lot of pipes and things which I finally realized stood for heating and wiring circuits. It all looked terribly technical.

'Very impressive,' I said. Impressive is the word I use when I don't understand something.

'Well, what do you think?'

Think? I looked more closely at one of them. It had a multifuel cooker which also did the heating and water, like the one that had never managed to heat Ryegill properly. 'Will it work?' I said for the sake of saying something.

'In a small house, it will. But I've gone off it.'

'Why?'

'The water's too acid around here – it eats through the pipes.'

'It hasn't eaten through mine.'

'Yours are all heavy gauge. It'll just take longer. Look at these two.'

I looked. The other one had been single-storey, but these seemed to have a basement at ground level. Barnaby explained that the multifuel boiler went there, along with fuel, workspace, utility area, car – whatever the client needed in his particular situation. The living area was above to allow for gravity warm-air heating. This meant no vulnerable pipework except to sinks and bath. It also meant no electricity in running it, though a client might wish to add a booster fan for quick heat. The 'stuff' he had ordered from the library would help him work out the physics of circulating the air efficiently without electricity. What he was doing, he said, was adapting an old-fashioned American system which the Americans had prematurely abandoned in favour of high tech.

Clever Barnaby. I was getting interested despite myself. None the less, my eye kept returning to the living areas. 'There's only one bedroom in this one,' I said. 'Even single people have visitors.'

Barnaby grunted. The only visitor he'd ever had – or almost had – was his sister who descended with husband and two children despite Barnaby's phoned protest that there was no room. I pictured the entourage sweeping into the derelict house and then sweeping out again in horror. When I say Barnaby's a loner, I'm not exaggerating. Still, he had made provision in one of the houses.

'No,' he said. 'That's a study.'

I thought of the disputed boxroom in which Andrew and I had spent so many uncomfortable nights. 'You might make it a little bigger,' I said, 'just in case.'

'How much bigger?'

We discussed this a while. Though he put up resistance (enlarging the room might unbalance the ducting system), he seemed to be listening. 'What exactly did you want my advice about?' I asked.

'The whole thing,' he said. 'I want your opinion. What I mean is, would you consider living in it?'

Was Barnaby proposing?

He was not. He meant, as always, exactly what he said.

The rest of the afternoon passed in detailed discussion of his designs. In a way, I was more flattered by his wanting my advice than I would have been by a proposal. It had been a long time since Andrew had asked my opinion. For that matter, since anyone had, not counting library business.

At one point I annoyed him by suggesting, as tactfully as I could, that, sound as his designs were, I couldn't see them wowing anyone at the Ideal Home Exhibition. The reaction was unexpected, explosive, and revealing. At last I understood. First the anti-hero, then the anti-novelist; and now, the anti-architect. Barnaby was designing houses for people who didn't like houses. He assumed his future clients had better things to do than fuss around trying to create an ideal home in which to do ... what? Ponder the ideal home? Barnaby's mythical client led a busy life subverting the status quo and wanted a house that wasn't forever demanding attention, a house that functioned so perfectly that its inhabitant could forget it existed. It was a startling idea, especially in our picturesque Arcadia where everyone's dream was a House With Character. Barnaby's house had no character except that which would be imposed on it by its owner. It could be built in a variety of materials to suit pocket and location. It was highly insulated and double glazed for both sound and heat. It was extremely cheap to run. It was the representation of Barnaby's credo that efficiency not only didn't dehumanize but actually made possible a fuller human existence. It was, in short, a miniature and humanized phoenix rising from the Bauhaus ashes.

'I see you've made another concession,' I said, pointing to one of the kitchens. Though the houses were designed for one or two people and had no dining room, the kitchens were large enough to seat four.

'I believe,' said Barnaby, 'that some people indulge in a peculiar activity called Entertaining at Home.'

I laughed. 'Come home with me tonight and be entertained. There's a casserole waiting to go into the oven.'

Barnaby looked alarmed.

'Alice and Diana are coming over,' I explained.

The alarm decreased only marginally.

'You were curious enough about them the other day.'

Barnaby came home with me.

I wish I could report an instant rapport with the four of us forming a weird but lovable ménage. Alice was easy (Alice likes everyone), but Diana and Barnaby never took to each other. We did go on one walk together on the fells surrounding the town. God knows how that came about but we never tried it again.

I also wish I could report that at the end of the first evening, when my neighbours went home, Barnaby and I fell into bed together. In fact, that didn't happen for some time, and even now, sex plays a relatively small part in our lives (except occasionally on the chamomile lawn). Barnaby isn't very highly sexed, and my own capacity for passion left when Andrew did.

There's never been any question of Barnaby moving in with me or me with him. We like our respective solitudes. What we lack in romance we make up for in companionship. We rarely talk about houses any more, or gardens, or other people's children.

Barnaby will never be rich and famous, nor will he revolutionize the countryside, let alone British society. But in his modest way he's doing what he can and is today up in the hills building his first house. He seems happy enough. So does his client.

24

The roses have come and nearly gone again. Who would have guessed that such a long cold spring would turn into a storybook summer? I like it much more than the roses do. They spent so long in the cold queue that when the heat came, so suddenly, it took them by surprise and, forgetting their English manners, they rushed into flower all at once.

Most of them are in the hedge planted by one of my predecessors. He certainly had an eye for roses. More to the point, he had a nose. Nearly all are fragrant, and even Mummy was surprised at the variety they yield to the nose. A rose by any other name does not smell as sweet. My Austrian Yellow is downright stinky, while others disguise themselves—Paulii, for example, as cloves, and my Spinosissima Double White as lily of the valley. But these tricksters are in the minority. Most of my roses smell like roses, from the fresh and sweet to the heavy exotic scents which evoke harems in walled gardens.

Every summer I play a childish game. I shut my eyes and walk along the hedge trying to identify each rose by its fragrance. I usually get it right, but even the most staid roses can sometimes be coy. They may go on strike in the morning, then release their scent in the afternoon. Or the other way around. They also smell different at different stages of blooming.

Another game I play is Flower Pseud. It began with my amusement at the word 'bouquet' used for wines (sour grapes, if you'll pardon the pun; I am no wine expert). I retaliate with pretentious descriptions of rose fragrances. For example, Blanc Double de Coubert: the sleek, sophisticated and slightly dangerous aroma of white satin against a courtesan's shoulder.

I also used to play Desert Island Roses, but now that divorce threatens my own modest Eden this game has become too poignant.

So I sit beside the hedge and breathe in the slightly rank smell of roses who have had their day. I'm trying to order the events – some of them very recent and very ugly – which have led to my precarious present. For this I return yet again to the past, this time to Camille's.

25

Camille had been an easy-going and considerate person until the birth of her two children. It's tempting to conclude that motherhood didn't suit her, but she would probably argue that no one can cope alone with the strain of raising children while holding down a full-time job. True, she had a child-minder, plus a great deal of help from Mike, me and various friends. But she felt so passionately about the right of every mother to free pre-school facilities that having to pay her child-minder destroyed the peace of mind she would otherwise have gained from her freedom.

The obvious solution was to leave her job. This she refused to do for two reasons: (a) financial necessity (though Mike disagreed); and (b) an equally passionate conviction that every mother has a right to a full-time job. She wished to set an example for the less enlightened women in our town.

But it soon became clear to those who knew her well that she was heading for a nervous breakdown. At this point – somewhere in the mid-seventies – I intervened.

The scene took place at the greengrocer's where we ran into each other during a quick lunch-time shopping. Not as quick as we'd hoped – there was a queue. While waiting her turn, Camille made some remark about all the vegetables pumped up with chemicals (her own gardening was organic but there were a few things she still had to buy). I agreed.

Our conversation proceeded from agricultural pollution to nuclear waste and thence to nuclear weapons.

'It's odd,' I said, 'how nobody seems to worry about the bomb any more.'

Camille pondered my sentence and a grapefruit at the same time. 'Yes...' she said slowly.

'It's almost as if nuclear waste has taken over from CND,' I continued.

She looked up from the grapefruit. 'You're right,' she said. 'Do you think it's a plot?'

We both laughed, and then we stopped laughing. Neither of us liked conspiracy theories, but suddenly it did seem a little odd.

'Not that nuclear power isn't just as big a problem,' said Camille. She put the grapefruit back and we moved up one in the queue.

'Of course.' I picked up the grapefruit. Chemicals or no, I fancied one. 'But the bombs are still being made.'

Camille stared at me and then at the window. People were hurrying past through the rain. There was nothing to see, so I knew she was thinking. 'Jesus,' she said quietly. 'Where've I been all these years?'

I remembered her homesickness for political action in 1968. We'd been earthing up spuds at the time. I nearly said, 'Earthing up spuds and having babies.' Then I had a thought. The idea must have been lurking in my mind without my knowing it, for the plan unfolded with remarkable speed and clarity. 'Doing social work for the slightly less privileged,' I said.

It was true. Camille's clients, compared with their urban counterparts, were scarcely in need of her help. Mildly delinquent children, an occasional neglected baby, marriages which might have broken down more peaceably on their own. I wasn't being nasty – Camille herself often expressed doubts about the value of her work in this most privileged corner of Britain.

'Yes . . .' she said again. Then she frowned at me. 'What *is* CND up to these days?'

I shrugged and moved up to the counter and busied myself with my purchases. The timing couldn't have been better.

A few months later I was filing cards and looked up to see Camille smiling at me across the catalogue. This wasn't unusual. She often popped in between clients to leave a message or collect a parcel or even sometimes to borrow a book. What was unusual was her smile, an impish one I remembered so well from childhood. I'd missed it the last few years.

'Hi, sister,' she said.

'Is that feminist or family?'

'Both.'

I slotted another card in and went on to the next drawer. 'Out with it,' I said. 'You're wearing your announcement face.'

'I'm going back to part-time next month.'

'By choice?'

She pretended to be annoyed. 'Of course. I'm extremely valuable.'

'What are you going to do with all that nice new free time?' I asked, though I already had a pretty good idea.

'Work for CND.'

'Fantastic!'

'I'm going to start a local branch – try to keep the issue alive.' She looked around my somnolent library. 'Or rather, put some life back into it.'

We both laughed, though I felt slightly disloyal towards my borrowers. Who could blame them? To people brought up among timeless hills and an equally timeless social system, the bomb must seem a laughable upstart, just another plaything in the politicians' toy-chest. 'What does Mike think?'

'Very keen. Actually, he worked out that financially it'll hardly make any difference.'

'How's that?' The catalogue is a high one and the way Camille was slouching her head looked like a jolly little pumpkin placed on it for decoration.

'Mrs Sproat was about to put her prices up.'

'I don't follow.'

The pumpkin frowned, impatient with its obtuse sister. 'Mrs Sproat. You know, our child-minder.'

'Camille, I know who Mrs Sproat is.'

'Well, we won't need her any more, will we!'

I'd hoped, of course, to shed my own child-minding day, but I couldn't really object. By then Emma had started school, and Dominic was so much easier that sometimes as I pottered about the garden on my day off, I almost forgot he was there. At any rate, Camille was easing my own social conscience. I agreed with her that everything she did for CND she also did for me. True, she did not work for CND on the day I looked after the children. But paying for Mrs Sproat had always been an ideological as well as a financial niggle; freed from it, she changed dramatically. The aggression and righteous indignation that had disfigured her for years disappeared. This made life so much pleasanter that it seemed good exchange for a day of babysitting. Our parents were delighted, too. So was Mike.

I don't know which was the main cause of this miracle: the dismissal of Mrs Sproat or the involvement with CND. What I do know is that Camille is a born politician. By the early eighties, when CND made its comeback, our town had one of the highest per capita memberships in the country. Given the conservative nature of the area, this was as much a miracle as Camille's own transformation.

I like to think back and imagine it all started with that tiny conversation at the greengrocer's.

26

If the day of the greengrocer's was one turning point in Camille's life, the day of the downspout was another.

That was the autumn of 1978. Andrew had just moved to London, Barnaby had just revealed his midget houses, and I was slowly adjusting to my solitary state.

I forget whether it was a nephew or the son of a friend who violated the downspout – so many children have come and gone that I lose track. I have a dim memory of some small male trying to climb it and bringing both it and himself down in a heap. (Is the tendency of small children to climb everything in sight a remnant of our monkey ancestry?)

Barnaby was horrified. He disapproved of water in all but a few places (bathtub; sea) and painted a terrifying picture of evil-minded rivulets boring their way under the house and destroying the foundations. He was so horrified that he gave up a Sunday to repair it.

It was late September and we were harvesting the spuds. Now that I think of it, the oboist must have happened rather suddenly, for Andrew had dug his vegetable garden ready and then flitted before planting a thing. I remember Diana (who had no sympathy for my plight) eyeing the patch enviously. Her own self-sufficiency programme was progressing, but bringing a derelict garden into good heart is a slow process and she was short of cultivated land. Alice the mediator suggested, as tactfully as she could, that it would be a shame for all Andrew's elbow grease to be wasted. I agreed. We went shares on the seed spuds and turned the whole patch over to them.

And now, the harvest.

'Beige gold!' cried Diana as she lifted the first forkful.

Hidden treasure, buried doubloons. I wondered why Andrew had never planted spuds.

I, as librarian, catalogued and classified: damaged spuds, good spuds, Alice's, Diana's, Holly's spuds. I must have looked a proper earth mother again, sitting tailor-fashion on the patio as Diana gently tipped bucket after bucket of offerings in my lap.

Diana was never so happy as when she was digging – she loved all rough work. But I suspect there was another reason she banished herself to the potato patch that day: Barnaby, fixing the downspout while Alice played the role of his Sunday-absent 'lad'. For a radical feminist, Alice was surprisingly tolerant of Barnaby. I could hear her amiable chatter and even some responses from him. But Diana's hatred of men was total. No amount of good will and effort could make up for that missing X chromosome as far as she was concerned. Barnaby had the sense not to take it personally.

The gate squeaked (Barnaby wanted to oil it but I have a weakness for squeaky gates) and around the corner came Camille. She stood before us, hands on hips, smiling at us in silence.

I was used to her games. 'Tea?' I said.

She nodded.

I went in the house and made tea. When I returned, she was crouched over the spuds. 'Ours are lousy this year,' she said. 'Too many visitors. They love playing the rustic but somehow that doesn't run to tending spuds.'

'You can have some of mine,' I said.

The potato patch was screened by a row of potentillas.

Their foliage was tatty and touched with autumn but that didn't stop them flowering. Diana's torso rose above the innocent yellow flowers with a grace she would have despised if she'd known. 'Tea!' I called to her. It was obvious that Camille wouldn't make her announcement without the complete audience.

Diana tipped her bucket-load and sat down on the patio. Alice and Barnaby joined us. I poured the tea. 'All right,' I said, handing Camille her mug, 'what's your news?'

'I just posted a letter.'

Alice put down her mug and applauded.

'Very funny,' said Camille.

'I cut my toenails this morning,' said Diana.

'I opened a new bottle of grapefruit juice,' I said.

'I did the dishes,' said Alice.

Barnaby pondered a moment. 'I trimmed my beard.'

'Are you all quite finished?' said Camille.

We nodded.

'The letter was to my employers. Announcing my intention to terminate my employment.'

'Ah. Well. Yes. That is news,' I said. 'What precipitated the rash act?'

'A sudden and overwhelming sense of urgency. It occurred to me that if we don't get rid of these bombs soon, there aren't going to be any social workers. Or spuds. Or downspouts. I want to devote myself to CND.'

Diana nodded approvingly.

'What does Mike say?' I asked.

Diana frowned. (I should have sensed trouble.)

'He's all for it,' said Camille.

'And what about work equals money equals value?'

'I'm not too happy about it,' Camille admitted. 'But if Mike and I agree that what I do is valuable, I guess that's all that matters.'

'What's Mike got to do with it?' said Diana.

It was a silly question and Camille's answer was commendably mild. 'I do live with him.'

I should say here that mine wasn't the only consciousness being raised. Camille had recruited Diana for CND and was in turn being recruited as a feminist. This wasn't entirely new; Camille had always considered herself liberated. But now, under Diana's tuition, she was beginning to wonder just how liberated she was. This came out on a number of occasions when she made an uneasy fourth in our witches' kitchen of unmarried females.

Diana humphed softly and started to sort spuds. I noticed she put a damaged one in the wrong heap. I couldn't bear the thought of it rotting the others and removed it.

'Does this mean I can have my free day back again?' I said.

Camille didn't reply at once. I guess she'd hoped I would forget about that. 'I suppose so,' she said at last. 'Mike's willing to look after the kids more now.'

'Big of him,' said Diana.

'Diana . . .' I warned.

'Well, they're half his, aren't they? Does he do half the work?'

'He works full-time,' said Camille. 'And now that I won't be working at all, I can hardly expect—'

'Not working at all? Just because you won't be paid? You just said he agreed that what you're doing is valuable. Tell him to put his muscle where his mouth is.'

'He does help a lot,' said Camille.

'Like what?'

'He helps with the washing up. He does a lot of the garden and repairs and things.'

'And you don't?'

'Well, sure, but—'

'Who does the cooking?' Diana demanded.

'Mostly me, but—'

'And the laundry?'

'Well—'

'Who cleans the house?'

Camille laughed. 'Nobody!'

'Never?'

'Well . . .'

I was beginning to feel sorry for Barnaby, subjected to this onslaught on his sex. 'Barnaby does all these things for himself,' I said, 'and nobody gives him any praise for it.'

'He wouldn't if he had a female slave.'

Why didn't I shut up?

'Hey, you leave Barnaby out of it,' said Alice.

Diana glared at her and it occurred to me, belatedly, that this whole performance was being put on not for Camille but for Alice. Diana was jealous! Heaven knows why. Alice was just being friendly in her charming and indiscriminate way. I looked at the potentilla flowers nodding away in the breeze and willed Diana back behind them. That being impossible, I asked if anyone would like more tea.

Alice laughed. 'Holly thinks all the world's problems can be solved by a cup of tea.'

Dear Alice! 'It's an ancient English cure,' I said as I poured. 'You ought to know by now.'

The conversation wandered and with it my mind so that somehow I failed to hear the resumption of Diana's campaign. Then I caught the end of a sentence. Camille was sounding awfully defensive:

'. . . and that he'd look after them in the evenings.'

'How long's an evening?'

'Pardon?'

'And how long is a day? Call that fifty-fifty?'

'I didn't call it anything.'

'How can you let him get away with it? He gets you to have his kids and then makes like Father Bountiful because he looks after them a few hours a night!'

Camille said nothing. How could she? She'd been the one who wanted the kids. Not that Mike needed persuading.

Diana seemed to interpret the silence as capitulation. At any rate, she softened her voice. 'Camille, you're letting the side down.'

Camille wasn't the only one who knew how to manipulate people. That softened voice and the use of Camille's name was far more devastating than all the previous rants. Camille looked suitably chastened.

I had to defend her.

'No marriage is fifty-fifty,' I said.

'You can say that again!' said Diana.

'I don't think any relationship is.'

'No?' She looked at Alice. I expected Alice to refute it with a joke. To my surprise, she didn't. Perhaps equality *was* possible if you began equal? A startling thought. Then I noticed Camille. She was watching the couple intently. Judging by her face, she was thinking the same thing.

27

And so began the fifty-fifty plan. As Camille explained to Mike, a relationship of total equality would make them almost unique among married couples. Perhaps that tickled his vanity. No, that's not fair. Mike was a decent sort of guy. He had genuine liberal feelings and no affection whatsoever for the blatant mcps who naturally dominate such towns as ours. But he also had a tremendous competitive drive (remember, he taught PE) and a will to succeed. I think he saw the new regime as a game which the Mike/Camille team could and should win.

The first problem was to establish the rules. As the idea was to share all work equally, a definition of 'work' had to be found.

Work: that which it is unpleasant to do. On the whole, Mike liked his teaching and Camille her CND work, so that one was scrapped.

Work: that which one would not do if one were not paid for it. Camille wasn't paid for her CND work, so that had to be scrapped, too. In the end, they decided to exclude both the teaching and the CND, as they cancelled each other out anyway. All remaining activities were subjected to the following definition.

Work: that which one would not choose to do if one could choose to do something more desirable in the equivalent time. That was pretty good. Though neither found gardening 'unpleasant', they would happily exchange an hour of digging for an hour of walking on the fells.

The resulting items officially designated 'work' were listed and shared out equally. In some cases (cooking, laundry, cleaning) they did alternate weeks. With child care a more sophisticated system had to be worked out because Mike couldn't look after the kids while he was at school and hence got nearly all the evenings, weekends, and holidays. That left a miscellany of unequivalent jobs (Camille staking the peas versus Mike repairing the car) in which the time taken per job was written down and a weekly totting up done with suitable adjustment for the injured (i.e. overworked) party.

It all seemed terribly complicated but they seemed to thrive on it, at least at first. As I've said before and must stress again, Camille was by nature an easy-going and cheerful person. She ate Mike's first experimental meals without complaint, laughed off the occasional scorched blouse, and cared little whether Mike scrubbed the floors as efficiently as she did. For his part, Mike felt in the vanguard of fashion and boasted of his new accomplishments.

And yes, it was always Mike learning Camille's old chores, never the other way around. Eventually Mike noticed. When he mentioned this to Camille, she went over the figures with him again. It was, as she claimed, strictly fifty-fifty. The discrepancy, she said, was due to the fact that in the past she had done more than her fair share. Mike accepted this for a while but, once raised, the suspicion remained lurking under the surface. It erupted occasionally in bursts of irritation. This in turn led to rows. After one of them, Mike came to see me.

It was autumn again, about a year after the fifty-fifty plan went into action. I was planting out the wild sweet violets I'd grown from seed the previous winter. A happy job, this, and certainly not 'work' – no way did I want to be doing anything else. With my tray of peat pots balanced against one hip, I wandered the paths seeking congenial homes for the newcomers. A little clump here, an odd one there to look as if it had strayed in by chance and found the natives friendly and stayed. The soil exuded that Indian Summer smell that's so like spring, and in my imagination I combined it with the fragrance the flowers themselves would someday produce. I was singing the Lavender Cry from the Vaughan Williams symphony, substituting sweet violet and confident of my magic garden solitude. I hadn't heard the gate squeak. I looked up, mid-phrase, to see Mike and Dominic.

They didn't look very pastoral. Mike's irritation had transmitted itself to Dominic who broke away and ran off to some hidden corner to do God knows what damage. So much for Arcadia.

'What can I do for you?' I said briskly.

'Talk to Camille.'

It sounded so peculiar, coming like that. What did he think I did – sang to Camille? Shouted at Camille?

'What about?' I asked.

He explained. Camille was going to be away the whole of next week, instructing some people on how to set up their own CND branch. She'd arranged for the children to go home with school friends and await collection by Mike.

'So?' I said. It sounded reasonable enough.

'She's counting those five days as hers.' How, he asked, could she count as 'hers' days when she wasn't even there? What's more, he was the one who would have to get the kids up and off to school those five mornings.

I saw his point.

Further, he went on, now that Dominic had also started school, it was hardly fair that the hours of school custodianship counted as 'work' for Camille.

I saw that point, too, but I didn't want to be involved.

'Why don't you explain to her what you just explained to me?' I suggested.

'I did. She wouldn't listen.'

'So why should she listen to me?'

'You're her sister.'

'You're her husband.'

'Hah!'

That sounded bad. Even so, I was reluctant to interfere and I resisted vigorously. What finally persuaded me was the invitation to dinner. It was Camille's week for cooking and that night she was doing fish-and-garlic pie, one of my favourites that had been deleted from my own repertoire now that I was solo. If I would just have a word with her after the meal . . .

After the meal, we retired to her little study while Mike kept an eye on Dominic. Camille put her case. She'd had to make all the arrangements for the kids to go home with school friends – surely that counted as work? As for the school custodianship, what Mike had omitted to say was that both kids also spent a considerable amount of evening and weekend and holiday time (that is to say, Mike's time) with friends. Indeed, Emma was spending that very night with a friend so they could watch some television programme (television was banned from Ryegill).

Well, I could see her point. After our conference, I brought the two sides together and suggested that their various points seemed equally valid and they might therefore wish to consider the disputed week 'neutral'.

The reaction was far from neutral. I listened, horrified, to the resumption of hostilities. Figures and calculations whizzed past me from both sides. At last I stood up. The figures ceased. They were both looking at me as if expecting a revised ruling.

'You are looking,' I said, 'at a woman with a failed

marriage. I am in no position to give advice on anyone else's. I apologize for having attempted to do so. I will not repeat the mistake.'

And I left.

I wasn't drawn into their disputes after that. The disputes, however, didn't stop. Indeed, they became more frequent. The reason was that CND discovered Camille's genius for organizing other people and asked her to help set up new branches all over the country. These periods away from home upset the fragile equilibrium demanded by the fifty-fifty plan. It would have required a very subtle mind indeed to distribute equality in their irregular lives, and when I was next approached, I pointed out that mine was not such a mind. In this way I avoided direct intervention. What I couldn't avoid was the abuse each delivered in the other's absence. My picture of this period is of being followed around the house and garden and library and shops by two evilly whispering shadows.

The whispering stopped in the spring of 1980. Almost exactly two years after Andrew left me, Mike left Camille. I hesitate to mention the circumstances, but, improbable as it may seem, I must record that when Mike left Camille he took up residence in the same flat and with the same oboist who had enticed Andrew away. Perhaps she had a fixation about our family.

It turned out to be a bad tactical error as far as Mike was concerned. Andrew's adultery had been balanced by having an unnatural wife who refused to give him children. Mike had no such excuse. Camille's reaction was swift and decisive. In an extremely bloody court case she divorced him for adultery and received a settlement commensurate with an abandoned mother of two young children. Ryegill remained hers, and the alimony was sufficient to maintain it with only a slight reduction in the standard of living.

Mike was pretty bitter about it all. No doubt this bitterness affected his love life. He soon left to take up another job in a comprehensive down south.

Camille was outraged. Part of the reason for her generous settlement was the equally generous access she had allowed Mike. When he left, her most reliable child-minder was gone. The thing had come full circle. Once again she had what amounted to a full-time, albeit unpaid, job. Once again she had to find child-minders. Once again I was called into service.

I could have murdered that oboist.

28

And still the summer goes on, and still the heat: in the evenings great billows of it prowling my garden like some kind of archaic animal seeking to avoid the shafts of night-cold that spear it in hidden dank places. I walk through it all, refusing to take sides, enjoying the abruptness of change.

On evenings like this it's hard to care that Dominic broke my record player and Andrew took the telly. I sit on a day-warmed rock and tune in to another channel. Sound-track courtesy of an aspen, its neat round blue-green leaves putting to shame the most intricate oriental wind chimes. Behind and a little to one side, a whitebeam provides a visual counterpart: its own leaves, downy white beneath, wink a comic come-hither to a sober rhododendron who is, at any rate, rooted to its place across the fence on the squire's land. I laugh out loud and a trespassing cat looks up from stalking who-knows-what. I should chase him out (I, a lover of birds), but his face is as comic as the whitebeam's fruitless flirtation and only makes me laugh again. Such seriousness in nature!

Nature? I planted the aspen, my predecessor the whitebeam, the squire (or his gardener) the rhododendron. The cat is someone's pet, and I am human.

A spray of late evening sun has escaped a Blake painting to explode on my face. I blink and remember Daddy.

29

When Camille and I walked into the hospital that day, we saw nothing but artifice: the clean white walls, the gleaming chrome and plastic of machinery no less complicated than the cockpits of the planes he used to fly, the scrubbed nurses with their efficient smiles, the red-white-and-blue bunting strung along the corridor. Even the flowers in his room looked plastic, though they were from Mummy's own garden.

She had put him in the private wing of an NHS hospital. This infuriated Camille, not because she begrudged him the money but because she had genuine ideals. These extended even to her own family, a point which needs to be made. I've often noticed, for example, that 'liberals' who support comprehensive education none the less slip into those districts with reputable grammar schools as soon as their children reach school age. Not so Camille. And her support of the NHS was equally fervid. She glared with undisguised hostility at the privilege surrounding her father.

I later learned that Daddy had sent only for me. Mummy assumed it was drug-induced amnesia and summoned Camille as well. I don't think it was meant to be a 'last visit' – death is now as well planned as birth and can be postponed to suit the survivors' convenience – so there was no sense of urgency as we entered the room together.

I was prepared for Daddy to look awful, and he did. Wasting diseases seem to love big people and carve them up with special delight. I hardly recognized him without all his surplus flesh but, like Camille, I concealed my horror, though probably not enough.

Hospital visits are a strange ritual. We talked about the weather. We talked about the Royal Wedding due to take place the following week. We talked about the solar panels Camille was thinking of having installed at Ryegill. We talked about Emma and Dominic but not Mike or Andrew. We did not talk about death, disease or hospitals except for a few comments on the food. If I hardly recognized Daddy's appearance, I recognized even less of his character in the silly old man mouthing platitudes from his crisp white pillow. I felt angry and abandoned. For a moment I thought they'd killed Daddy and put this impostor in his place – all a part of the service if you go private. I was so furious I could scarcely speak and let Camille do most of the talking.

About fifteen minutes before the end of the visiting hour Daddy asked if he could talk to me alone. Camille was only slightly surprised. (Remember, Daddy was mine and Mummy is Camille's.) I watched her leave. When I turned back, I was shocked to see that Daddy had put away his plastic smile and gained another ten years. He was now very, very ancient, but at least he was Daddy.

'Hollyhock,' he said, 'I'm dying.'

'Nonsense. The doctor says you're making good progress.' It was a phrase Mummy kept using and I repeated it without thinking.

Daddy shut his eyes. I wondered if he was going to sleep in revenge for my stupid sentence. 'Holly,' he said (I missed the diminutive), 'I only play these games to please your mother.'

I nodded, forgetting that his eyes were closed. He opened them to check up on me and now I saw that he was looking at me for the first time during the visit. I felt nervous and wasn't sure I didn't prefer the impostor.

'I want you to do something for me,' he said. There was another long pause. The pain he'd hidden from Camille was now visible, running about and doing its ugly work beneath the skin of Daddy's face. 'I want you to get me some drugs,' he said.

It seemed a strange request, in this building which was stuffed to the rafters with every kind of magic potion.

'I don't know which ones,' he continued. 'But Beattie will know.'

I wondered if his mind was wandering and I nearly said that Beattie was no nurse and knew nothing of such things. Then I remembered. Beattie belonged to the Voluntary Euthanasia Society. She did know about drugs, at least about those that extinguished life. And suddenly I realized what Daddy was really asking. He was asking me to help kill him. I looked away and willed Camille to return or a nurse to blunder in or, best of all, the impostor to come back with his plastic smile and jaunty quips.

'You have a lot of pain?' I asked. I hadn't meant to ask because I didn't really want to know.

He nodded. 'Even with the pain killers. And then my mind goes.'

I didn't know what to say and Daddy wasn't making it any easier, just staring at me and waiting for an answer. I'd almost forgotten the question. Daddy reminded me.

'Will you do that for me? Go to Beattie?'

I nodded automatically. Hadn't I always done what Daddy asked? Then I realized what my gesture meant. I had, without thinking, promised to help kill my father. How could he ask such a thing of me? Why hadn't he sent for Beattie? I felt as full of resentment for this demanding father as I had for the impostor before. 'Why don't you send for Beattie?' I said.

'Your mother wouldn't let me.'

I didn't know if that meant he'd tried and failed or given up without trying. Either way, I was still stuck with my promise.

'I'm sorry to do this to you, Hollyhock.'

The pet name was back when I least wanted it.

'I wouldn't ask,' he went on, 'if it didn't matter so much. Anyway . . .' There was another long pause. I suspected his mind was wandering. He shut his eyes again and I imagined him concentrating so hard on remembering just one little thing. I hoped it was worth it.

'Anyway?' I prompted.

He opened his eyes and looked at me as if I were a stranger. It was the most awful look I have ever received, and even now as I write I see it more clearly than any other memory of my father.

'Daddy?'

He continued to stare at the stranger who was me. I wondered if I should remind him who I was, but that seemed such an insult.

I bore the weight of that look for a very long time. I now know that the various drugs inside him worked like little time-clocks. They'd been set to bring him back to life for the allotted hour, but someone had mistimed and they'd switched off a little too soon.

'Why don't you go to sleep?' I said.

He shut his eyes obediently. Perhaps he'd got used to taking instructions from the nurses.

A nurse came in. 'Visiting hour is over,' she said with a smile. (The smile was what you paid extra for.) She came over to the bed. 'Sleeping peacefully?' she said.

'Yes.' It seemed to be part of the ritual. I went to the door. As I was closing it, I saw the syringe. All those drugs he was entitled to, but not the ones he wanted. For those, he had to make me a murderer.

I went back to the house and packed my case. I'd intended to stay the whole weekend but was glad to get away. The night before had been a travesty of a reunion: all the happy family gathered together minus a few husbands.

Luckily, Mummy was out, but there was still Camille. I told her I'd just remembered a meeting I had to attend the following day. She accused me of being an unnatural daughter. I agreed and left.

Driving north, I went over the conversation with Daddy. To be honest, I was looking for a loophole. I thought maybe that 'Anyway' contained one. *I wouldn't ask if it didn't matter so much. Anyway* ... But everything I filled in went against me:

Anyway, your mother would know what I was up to if I asked to see Beattie.

Anyway, you're my daughter, you owe me something. Beattie doesn't. But she'll do it for you.

Anyway, you're the only one who cares enough to stop me becoming a vegetable.

Anyway, I trust you.

There was no bunting on Beattie's street. The whole area was a university ghetto, though I did notice a poster of Lady Di in one or two windows. I parked outside the house and hurried up the steps and rang the bell. These small actions, after the frustrating hours imprisoned in the car, were a great relief.

Somewhere along the M1 a change had taken place. I'd ceased thinking of the moral dilemma and, without intending to, slipped into Daddy's place. I imagined myself lying there day after day hooked up to those machines and attended by bland well-meaning nurses and visited by relatives who on seeing the helpless patient themselves reverted to helpless childhood and its talismanic phrases like The-doctor-says-you're-making-good-progress when everyone knew damn well he was dying. I imagined what it was like knowing he was dying but having to keep up this awful pretence with his weak-willed relatives, i.e. me. I imagined how lonely it must be, dying all alone because no one would let him talk about it. And above all, knowing he would become a vegetable and say and do things that would disgrace his previous and already-dead self.

I was so busy imagining these things all over again that I failed to notice the obvious: no one was answering the door.

A tweed jacket and pipe and briefcase were making their way up the street. I recognized him from the English Department. More to the point, I recognized him as Beattie's next-door neighbour. It seemed a wonderful omen (I was beginning to think in omens) and I greeted him with excessive enthusiasm. He seemed puzzled though polite – clearly he didn't recognize me as either his former student or Beattie's niece. When I explained who I was, he rescued himself with grace, then told me Beattie was away.

Away?

At a conference in the States, he explained.

The extraordinary thing was, I had known it. I'd even asked Beattie to bring back a particular book for me. I knew, too, that after the conference she was spending a fortnight travelling around seeing old friends. All those hours driving and I hadn't once thought of the possibility that Beattie might not be there, and yet *I'd known*. The bad omen cancelled out the good and left me standing by the door in a state of shock. My only thought was that I had to get into the house. Somewhere in Beattie's house was the answer to what Daddy needed even if Beattie wasn't there to give it.

'Is anyone else home?' I asked. A stupid question, as no one had answered the door.

The lecturer said he didn't know. They were mainly graduate students, so someone might be around. He seemed slightly suspicious.

'I left something the last time I was here,' I lied. 'I need it urgently.' I tried to think what I might have left that would need such urgent retrieval, but he didn't ask. University people are nice that way. I wondered if I could press my luck further. 'I don't suppose there's some other way of getting in?' I asked. 'You know, when students forget their keys or something?'

Suspicion again. Even university people have their limits. Breaking into houses was clearly one of them.

'If you'd care to wait inside?' he said, indicating his own house with its tantalizingly open front door.

I thanked him and said I'd wait in the car – that way I'd be able to see if anyone came. But the real reason was a horror of being polite to this polite man and his polite wife and three children while my head was full of murder.

As I sat in the car I tried to think what I would do once I got inside the house. Beattie was nearly sixty. She smoked and drank heavily. She belonged to the Voluntary Euthanasia Society. It seemed probable that she not only knew about drugs but had already stashed away her future release. It would be somewhere inside that house. All I had to do was get in and search. I wasn't sure how I'd recognize the pills – does arsenic look different from aspirin? Perhaps there'd be a skull and crossbones on the bottle. I laughed nervously, then looked around to see if I'd been heard. There was no one. The street was deserted and smelled of dinnertime. That made me hungry, but I couldn't leave – what if a lodger returned in my absence and plugged himself into some headphones or, worse, left again?

There was nothing to eat in the car, nothing to read, nothing to do. Sometime during the evening I fell asleep. When I awoke, twenty minutes had passed. It seemed a gift. Surely someone had come home meanwhile? I hurried up the stairs again and rang the bell. The lecturer's head popped out of a window next door. He seemed surprised I was still there. I smiled cheerfully and returned to my car.

When it got dark, I got out of the car again and scrutinized the house in case there was a lighted window. There wasn't.

At midnight I gave up my vigil and drove home.

Now that it's over, I think of all the things I could have done. I could have gone to the medical library and looked up lethal dosages. I could have gone to my doctor and complained of chronic sleeplessness. Doctors expect that of women. I could have accumulated the pills and gone back to Daddy. I could even have returned to the hospital, learned where the drugs were kept, and stolen them.

And what did I do? I went home and carried on as normal. True, I tried phoning Beattie's house. For three weeks I tried. I must have worn out her phone trying. No one ever answered. By the time Beattie returned, Daddy was dead.

30

Camille and the children stayed with Mummy for a week after the funeral. I probably should have stayed too, but the way Mummy clung to her grandchildren I don't think she needed either of us – Camille just happened to be part of the package. I wasn't even that. Mummy's disapproval of me was by now so strong I scarcely felt I had a family at all.

Beattie invited me to stay with her a few days. I said I had to get back to work. That was true, but I also wanted to be alone. The bond with my father had been the first and, I suppose, the strongest. When he died, my capacity for all relationships died with him, at least for several months. I didn't even want to see Barnaby. The only people I could tolerate were those who didn't make any emotional demands. No one seeing me at the library would have guessed my father had just died. I was as cheerful as ever to my borrowers and staff.

Much later I learned that this virtue was interpreted quite differently by many people in town. From being an unnatural wife who refused to have children I progressed to being an unnatural daughter who refused to mourn her father. In a sense they were right. I was refusing to mourn. How could I mourn with Daddy's last weeks on my conscience? And how could I explain a guilt created by my failure to kill him? The only one who might have understood was Beattie, and she was too bound up with that failure.

It was several months before I could face the house where I'd held my stupid vigil. I took up Beattie's invitation, belatedly but with gratitude, after spending an awful family Christmas in London. Nothing seemed to have changed there. It was as if Mummy and Camille and Emma and Dominic had frozen into their post-funeral positions like four sleeping beauties awaiting some outsider to come and wake them up. I wasn't that somebody. I left them as I found them and fled to Beattie.

We got stupendously drunk the first night. At least, I got stupendously drunk; with Beattie you could never tell – she always seemed sober however much she drank. That night she was reclining on an ancient *chaise-longue* with a lodger's cat on her lap (she didn't mind pets as long as they were quiet). I was curled up in an ugly but extremely comfortable armchair. The only lamp on was an orange shaded one which cast a sense of warmth over the shabby room. A small old-fashioned Christmas tree in one corner provided a second source of light, while a lively coal fire made a third. We were drinking mulled wine. Outside the snow was blowing. It was that very snowy cold December of 1981 and I'd had a hard time driving north through a blizzard. I'd been greeted on arrival by a hot meal and sanity. And then the mulled wine, the cat, the soft warm light and the coal fire while outside the winter did its thing – and suddenly it felt like the Christmas that had bypassed us in London had finally arrived, a few days late but none the less welcome for that. Muscles which had been tensed for months relaxed and I felt myself melting into a dangerously soft pool of sentiment. But why dangerous? Here was Beattie, my ancient aunt confessor who had never let me down. I looked around the comforting room. The time was right.

'Daddy asked me to help kill him,' I said.

Beattie didn't reply. She just went on stroking the cat. Its purr was the loudest thing in the house.

'He asked me to get some drugs from you. I tried, but you were in the States. I tried phoning you for three weeks, but then he died.' I hadn't put it well. It sounded as if I were blaming her for not being there. I hoped she would understand that I was blaming myself.

At last she spoke. 'I'm sorry you had so much anxiety.'

'Anxiety?' It seemed a feeble word for guilt. Somewhere far off in the house I heard the scrape of a chair and a soft footstep – one of her lodgers was working straight through Christmas on his thesis. It was as comforting a sound as the cat. 'Beattie, would you mind if I told you the whole story?'

She peeled away the cat and stood up. 'Let me get you some wine first.' She went into the kitchen where the wine was keeping warm. There was a touch of formality in the way she refilled our glasses and settled herself in properly before I began. To anyone not knowing her it might have been off-putting. To me, it meant she expected a full account. It was exactly what I needed.

And so I told her everything, from the conversation with Daddy right down to the night of speaking. There weren't many facts. The completeness lay in my thoughts, and those I revealed in detail. I even revealed thoughts I hadn't known I had till then. I knew I was treating her like an analyst, hoping somehow to shift my guilt. I knew, too, that it was something one should never do to another person, but somehow it seemed permissible that night.

When I finished, I waited. I'm not sure what I expected, but as the minutes ticked by, I realized I hadn't quite finished. There was a question she was waiting for me to ask. I wasn't sure I wanted to know the answer, but I knew she wouldn't speak till I'd asked it. This wasn't a time for cowardice. I looked right into her beady little eyes. 'Would you have given me the drugs?'

She smiled. 'Why didn't you tell me this sooner? No, I wouldn't have given you the drugs.'

It sounded like an absolution. She had taken the guilt on herself. I shouldn't have queried it, but I did. 'Why not?'

She lit a cigarette. 'Holly, you really are a silly goose. Think about it.'

I thought about it. I still couldn't see why not.

She sighed. 'Holly, arsenic belongs to fiction. The only drugs I can get are barbiturates. It takes a lot of them to kill a person, and they take a long time to act. You need at least sixteen undisturbed hours. How would your father have found sixteen undisturbed hours in that hospital?'

I remembered all those bland efficient nurses, the doctors hurrying along the corridors, the auxiliaries, even the visitors — someone would have found him 'in time'. Poor Daddy. There was no way anyone could have helped him once he got into that hospital. His life was no longer his. He had no choice.

Beattie had disappeared. She returned with the saucepan of mulled wine. I was amazed there was any left.

'I still feel guilty,' I said. 'Daddy trusted me. All those weeks he was waiting and hoping I would do something, and I didn't. I let him down.'

Beattie shook her head. 'Not at all. You gave him the one bit of hope that still had meaning for him. Do you understand?'

I understood. This was no phony absolution or belated Christmas gift from my nice aunt. It was the real thing.

The following day I did some shopping while Beattie worked on a paper. She always had several papers on the go at once — I don't know how she kept them apart in her mind, but they seemed as necessary a drug to her as the whisky and cigarettes. I came back in time to see her crouching before a safe which I had mistaken for a little table. It was covered by a fringed cloth and on this occasion topped by the Christmas tree. I peered over her shoulder as she put her unfinished paper into the safe. Then I set down my parcels and laughed.

'What's so funny?'

'I've heard of industrial sabotage, but academic?'

'Fire,' she explained.

The safe was full of papers. The only other thing I could see was a bottle. I wondered if it was an emergency whisky bottle, but it was too small. I picked it up. It was unlabelled. It was full of pills.

'Are these the drugs?'

'Yes.'

There were an awful lot of them. I wondered how anyone could get them all down in time. How did you kill yourself if you were one of those people who couldn't swallow pills? I looked at Beattie and then at the pills that would result in a non-Beattie. It seemed extraordinary that those little pills could extinguish someone as tough as Beattie. It also seemed extraordinary that there would someday be a world without Beattie. I didn't want to think about it. If I did, I might have to think about a world without Holly, too. What a shoddy business mortality was. You got hauled into the world without anyone asking your permission, and then when you finally got used to it and started to like living, you got hauled out again.

Beattie took the bottle from me and put it back in the safe. 'If you want to be nosy, look at this instead.' She reached out a folder that wasn't one of her papers and handed it to me. On the cover were the words LAST WILL AND TESTAMENT. I tried to hand it back.

'These things are supposed to be secret,' I said.

'Why? Go on. Read it.'

'I thought wills were kept in solicitors' offices.'

'Mine is tired of me. I keep taking it back to make additions. He's got the second key to the safe. By the way, let me show you where I keep my own key.' She showed me – it was a very obvious place.

'Beattie, I don't like all this talk about death.'

She laughed and patted my head in passing. 'Come and read it in the kitchen.'

We went into the kitchen. Beattie started scraping carrots. My offer to help was declined, so I started to read. I suppose I was nosy, in a general sort of way. I'd never seen a will before. Wills were like butlers and revolvers: semi-mythical objects that belonged to novels, not real life.

The language was disappointingly dry and convoluted. When I finally deciphered it, I could see why Beattie's solicitor was fed up with her. The will consisted of a long list of items, mostly of little value, destined for an equally long list of people. There were also some complicated instructions to her literary executor – some professor I'd never heard of – about what to do with any unfinished manuscripts. The rest was fairly straightforward. Her books would go to the university library. Camille would get £1000. I would get the rest.

I stared at Beattie's back. It was quivering energetically to the motion of scraped carrots. I didn't know what to say. I would have preferred not to have known about the will. As things turned out, it would have been a blessing.

I put down the will and went to the sink and started peeling potatoes against Beattie's objections.

'You're my guest,' she said. 'You cook for me at your house, I cook for you here.'

I went on peeling potatoes. I'd never thought about Beattie's will. If I had, I would have assumed Mummy would get her estate. Or that it would be split equally between Camille and myself. 'Why have I been singled out?' I asked quietly.

She laughed. 'Why not?'

'You have two nieces,' I said. 'Camille will be hurt.'

Beattie started slicing the carrots. 'You overestimate Camille's sensitivity.'

'It'll look odd.'

'No doubt. Holly' — she stopped slicing and looked at me — 'there aren't many things I have control of in this life. My will is one of them. Let me do as I please.'

I didn't say anything. She finished slicing the carrots and put them into the growing stew. I added my potatoes. She put the lid on and got out the sherry bottle. We sat down at the kitchen table with our glasses. Beattie never looked at home in the kitchen, but her motions were more self-conscious than usual that day.

'I'm sorry if I've embarrassed you,' she said. 'In my first will I did divide it equally between you and Camille.'

'Why did you change it?'

'When Andrew left, you were on your own. It seemed only fair to redress the balance as far as I could.'

'Mike's left Camille,' I reminded her.

'Camille has alimony, two children, and a state that looks after mothers.'

'I have my job.'

'For how long? Holly, this isn't a recession. It's not even a depression — countries get out of depressions. It's not going to get out of this one.'

'My job is more secure than most.'

'Perhaps. I hope you're right. If not, you'll have something to fall back on.'

'What if the alimony stops? What will Camille have to fall back on?'

'The state will look after her as long as her children are dependants. When they grow up, they'll be expected to look after her. It may be unfair on the children, but that's how it works. Children are insurance policies. You and I don't have any. We have to look after ourselves.' She smiled. 'Why do you think I have those pills? Because

I don't have children to put me in a nice little granny flat.'

'You can come and live with me when you're old,' I said.

Beattie laughed. 'And have you despising your senile old aunt?'

I thought about the stranger disguised as my father. Then I thought about Mummy. With a terrible shock I saw the future. A granny flat at Ryegill? No. Mummy would live out her old age in comfort with me – the daughter she liked least. I pictured us, bickering daily, learning to hate each other. She would never take any pills. She would squeeze every last drop of life out of me rather than do anything so unnatural. And I would be unnatural if I refused to let her do so.

'The state isn't interested in single people,' said Beattie. 'Everything is structured around the family. Single people have to look after themselves. I'm lucky: I have my own house and I'll retire on a good pension. Isn't it reasonable that I should share my good fortune with another single person?'

I shook off the awful vision of my mother.

'Can I ask a hypothetical question?'

She nodded encouragement to her dim student.

'What if Camille were single and I had the two children?'

She got up and stirred the stew.

'I'm calling your bluff,' I said. 'Favouritism versus principle. Come on.'

She returned to the table and poured out more sherry for us both. Then she laughed. 'You see how lucky I am? I don't even have to choose.'

'You wouldn't let a student get away with that.'

'Very well. In the hypothetical case you so meanly put before me, I would probably divide my estate equally. Half favouritism, half principle.'

'Can I ask another question?'

She nodded more warily this time.

'Was I always your favourite niece?'

'You mean all those years when your mother kept leaving the two of you with me while I was trying to write my thesis? No. I detested you both. Does that shock you?'

I thought about my six nephews and nieces and all the other people's children who had been dumped on me for so many years. 'No,' I said. 'Not any more.'

31

Even storybook summers end and we in the north revert with good grace to a land of rain and wind. Here and there, a secret sigh of relief, perhaps. Eden is alien to us. Golden days sit better in fireside memory.

A lull lures me out for a quick breath of fresh air but I see from the tail of my eye some spent delphiniums that have blown over. They're squashing the michaelmas daisies. I go over and remove them and see a dock that escaped the autumn weeding. It's coming up beside a hypericum that's blooming despite the recent storms. A longer diversion, this; I have to go to the potting shed and get the fork to dig it out. I wonder how many other weeds have escaped me and I contemplate a serious tour of inspection. I picture my fig-leafed predecessors strolling about, trowel and fork in hand. A lot of acres for two people. I see them pause at the tree. Would I have eaten? Yes.

32

After Mike left (and despite the alimony), Camille's life became more difficult again. The scroungers (I may as well be frank) who drifted in and out of Ryegill always seemed to be drifting out when Camille needed them. Her CND work was erratic and unpredictable and needed a stable backdrop. Now her domestic life was equally erratic. The two clashed. Camille never knew from one day to the next what she would be doing or who would be looking after the children. She took downers at night and uppers during the day. Her body became as confused as her mind. Daddy's death and the strain of coping with Mummy immediately afterwards when I selfishly fled didn't exactly help.

In the spring of 1982 she began crying for no reason at all. She would be in a shop or cooking a meal or writing a business letter or even addressing a meeting when suddenly she would burst into tears. She couldn't explain why.

Finally she went to the doctor. We shared the same doctor, but with her he was always the infinitely gentle and sympathetic family practitioner. He was at his best when dealing with family crises. On this occasion he diagnosed Nervous Breakdown and prescribed a complete rest: Camille must take at least a week off and go somewhere that had no associations with either CND or family; she must go alone, take no work with her, do no work while there, and be looked after entirely by other people. I think he had in mind something like a German spa.

Camille's reaction was bitter. How could she, a mother of two, just drop everything and flit?

Her friends and relatives would understand, said the doctor. They would look after everything.

For us in the north, the five weeks preceding the 1982 May Day holiday were unusually dry. That meant Barnaby was unusually busy. That in turn meant that (a) he got a good head start on his summer building work, and (b) he wore himself out taking advantage of the endless rainless days. In an unwitting parody of the doctor (I knew nothing of the consultation), I prescribed a holiday for Barnaby and me.

Barnaby hated to take time off, but on this occasion, he relented. I think he knew that despite Beattie's assurances I still felt guilty about Daddy's death. A few days away would do us both good.

He had a friend in a Yorkshire seaside town whom he hadn't seen for years. The friend was particularly keen to see Barnaby because he'd just bought a tiny cliffside house which he wished to improve. Though Barnaby lived too far away to be his builder, the unbiased advice of an old friend seemed a good idea. Barnaby phoned him and the invitation was extended to include me.

I was terribly excited. I hadn't been to the town since a family holiday a few years after the war. Of all our holiday sites, it was the one I most vividly remembered. I don't know why I didn't think of revisiting sooner, but once things were in motion, I invested the proposed trip with all the aura of a treasure hunt.

A few days before we were due to go, Camille came around in a flap. She'd made all the arrangements for her therapeutic week and now the people who were supposed to look after Emma and Dominic had left. What was she to do? No one at Ryegill, Mike 'too tied up' to take them at such short notice, and Mummy incapacitated with the 'flu.

'I'm incapacitated, too,' I said. 'Barnaby and I are going away.'

Camille burst into tears.

The weather broke on the Saturday. Barnaby was rather pleased – it meant he couldn't have worked anyway. I was less pleased. Though he'd cleaned up the van (my car was too small for the four of us plus luggage), it was still a builder's van, and by the time we finished loading up in a freak blizzard, it had reverted to a muddy mess. The snow changed to hail when we set off. It bounced off the tinny roof like so many bullets, and twenty miles on I had a headache.

I was pretty edgy anyway. The treasure hunt had disintegrated into a hotel hunt. Barnaby's friend's house consisted of a living area, a bedroom, a bathroom, but even if he'd lived in a mansion, I wouldn't have imposed the kids on him like that. Too many people had done it to me. I'd suggested that Barnaby stay with his friend while I stayed with the kids at a hotel – we'd still be together during the day.

'Some holiday,' he'd said.

I saw his point.

Then I'd offered to pay his share of the hotel bill – after all, it was my fault he would have to stay in one at all.

No. Barnaby wasn't into charity.

'I'll just feel guilty,' I said.

'One of us has to.'

We tossed a coin. I lost.

Still, it was the coin's fault, not mine, and I shed my guilt about the time we stopped for lunch.

What a revelation! We might have been the Royal Family for all the fuss they made of us in that café. Special portions for the kids at special prices, smiles and merry chatter from the waitress (mother of three), benevolent looks from the other customers (parents all). I stared at Emma and Dominic to see if they'd metamorphosed; but no, still the same boring children as ever.

When we got to the town, same thing. The hotel proprietress, a big motherly lady (two of her own, grown up) couldn't have been nicer. Though by no means a grand establishment, it had a special children's room off the main lounge stuffed with toys and the promise of 'someone to keep an eye on the children' should we wish to wander off on our own.

I expected all this good will to evaporate as soon as we signed the register. Three surnames between the four of us was, after all, a bit peculiar. I explained the situation briefly (Barnaby became my 'fiancé').

No problem.

Well, I thought, maybe business is slack, what with the recession and the weather and all. Maybe she's making a special effort. But when we settled ourselves in and, during a break in the rain, went for a walk around town *en famille*, people kept smiling at us. I noticed they mainly had children the same age as Emma and Dominic. It was like Jaguar owners flashing their lights at each other. We were all in the same club.

The town had altered beyond recognition. I'd expected change, but even the streets had moved and I kept getting lost. On one corner my father's ghost beckoned me into a fishmonger's where we as children had marvelled at the strange smells and patterns of all the shellfish. I blinked and it turned into an antique shop. The town was full of them, and the high gloss of furniture polish dazzled my matt and sepia memories. A dusty little shop selling the local semi-precious stone had spawned half a dozen rivals and a showroom that wouldn't be out of place in London. There were boutiques, health food shops, craft centres of every description, and you couldn't take two steps without tripping over an artist painting yet again the picturesque harbour.

Still, it was picturesque, and my initial disappointment gave way to a strange sensation. You can't go back, no, but everywhere I looked Daddy imposed his image on the newness. I don't think I've ever felt as close to him as I did that afternoon. The damp sea breeze held more than the smell of fish and the cry of gulls. There was reconciliation in the air. I bowed my head for the benediction.

We ate as early as we could and installed the children in front of the telly under the watchful eye of the proprietress and half a dozen other mothers. We didn't ask them to look after the kids – I was determined never to do that to anyone – but they offered. The club again.

'Magic,' said Barnaby.

And off we went to see Barnaby's friend. I won't recount the evening as he plays no further role in this story beyond being the reason we went there rather than some other seaside resort. After the event it's easy to see all the ifs: if we hadn't gone to that particular town; if Camille hadn't taken her therapeutic holiday that week; if Mummy hadn't had 'flu; if Barnaby hadn't consented to a holiday; if we'd stayed at home as the children wanted; if I hadn't got cabin fever the next day and insisted on going for another walk.

33

It rained again the next day. There were gale force winds as well. The hotel was under siege, the high rooms echoing to the wails and whines of children deprived even of television because some nasty adults were watching the Open University of all things. In the children's room the toys were doing good trade, but everyone wanted the same item at the same time and there weren't enough comics to go around. The other residents seemed used to it, but to me it was an inferno.

By mid-morning I couldn't stand it any more and persuaded Barnaby that the rain had let up a little. The kids refused to come out at first, but when I shrugged and said they could stay in if they wanted, they changed their minds.

If only they hadn't. If only we'd gone to the museum instead, or the amusement arcade. If only the weather had been good and they'd played on the beach.

I was surprised at the number of people around. The quay was well dotted with other anoraks out of which peered other hardy souls. We watched the boats a while. There was an excursion that would have taken us out if the weather hadn't been so rough. Dominic tried to persuade the owner, but no luck. We compared fishing boats, Dominic choosing the one he'd like to own. We commented on the names. We imagined what it was like fishing out there in the middle of nowhere in such little boats. Daddy smiled at me from one of the cabins. I smiled back.

The full force of the wind hit us when we reached the pier. I clung to Barnaby. The kids, too old for human reassurance, clung to the green-painted rails. I should have felt nervous but didn't.

At the end of the old concrete pier was a lighthouse. I was glad we couldn't go in it. The thought of all that wind pushing at us from the top of a lighthouse was too much.

The pier continued in a newer wooden extension, but between the two sections was a broad catwalk with nothing but water and rocks beneath. There were eight or nine people on it, watching the huge swells come in and break on the rocks. We joined them. It was pretty spectacular. Even Emma lost her pubescent dignity and raced from one side to the other, following the progress of each wave and predicting how violent it would be when it crashed. Dominic was beside himself with joy. Their excitement surprised me – they'd always seemed such domesticated kids, far more interested in the artificial drama of television than the poor efforts of nature. The din was incredible. Even the squeals of the younger children were drowned out by the roaring smashing tons of water below. After a particularly big wave broke, a huge veil of water sprayed up and pattered onto the catwalk. I laughed aloud, no longer caring how wet I got. Barnaby laughed, too, though I could hardly hear him through the general uproar. I looked for Daddy, wanting to share it with him, but he wasn't there. I tried to remember if the catwalk and extension had existed all those years ago. Perhaps not. So many little seaside towns had merged and muddled my mind.

Dominic dashed across the catwalk and slipped. Barnaby caught him just before he would have landed on his rump. I should have been nervous but wasn't.

We moved on to the extension and started walking. There was nothing at the end of it but piers are compulsive that way, you have to walk to the end of them. This one was a double-decker, with a matching layer below. There was no one on the lower part – it was awash.

We got to the end and stared out across grey water towards a grey sky with no discernible horizon. I thought I saw a passing freighter but perhaps not – the foghorn further down the coast was bellowing away, so visibility must have been low. Thousands of miles away the *Belgrano* was being sunk. Nearer to home Camille was remembering that Argentina was within four years of having the bomb. Nearer still, Emma was draped over the railing looking very bored. Her elbow collided with Dominic's. Dominic pushed it away. Angry words. A squabble was imminent, so I steered my little 'family' back down the extension.

It was nearly lunchtime. We would eat somewhere and then, if the weather didn't lift, we'd go to the museum. Otherwise we'd go to the abbey, as we hadn't had time to see it the day before.

I took Barnaby's arm. Rain was dripping off his beard but he looked contented. Not so the children. The elbow incident had escalated, and every stretch of railing was claimed by either Emma or Dominic as sovereign territory. This meant a lot of dashing back and forth, barely missing some of the other tourists who were making their way up the extension – we seemed to be going against the traffic. One man dodged to avoid Dominic and nearly slipped on the wet wooden slats. Dominic didn't notice. He was hurtling towards the seaward rail just ahead of Emma. The man who'd nearly been knocked down scowled at me in passing. I didn't blame him. I shouted at the children to stop, that they were being a nuisance and anyway it was too slippery for all this running. I must have looked away for a second because all I remember is a blur, a scream, then more screams, and when I looked at where Dominic had been heading there was no Dominic.

34

The inquest was brief, a formality. There was no suggestion of blame. The coroner praised Barnaby's rescue attempt as heroic. If he'd known that Barnaby couldn't swim he might have called it idiotic. Even Barnaby doesn't know how he survived. I think the tide was coming in and must have helped him as he groped his way to shore with his burden that was already past saving. Someone on the beach tried the kiss of life and was also singled out for praise. Luckily, there'd been quite a few witnesses, all with similar evidence.

None of this helped either Dominic or me.

Camille was very decent, given that I'd just killed her only son. Her dry eyes at the funeral were seen as stoic. Mine, I discovered later, were interpreted differently.

Mummy was beside herself. I never knew how apt the phrase was till I saw her at the funeral. You would have thought Dominic was her son, not Camille's. 'My only grandson! My only grandson!' she kept moaning and looking at me accusingly – whether because I hadn't produced any other grandson or because I'd killed off the one she had I don't know.

Mike was also there but there was no question of reconciliation.

Barnaby was still recovering from some sort of pneumonia and couldn't attend the funeral, but Beattie was there. Afterwards she came home with me. She was with me when I opened the large unaddressed envelope someone had slipped through the letterbox in my absence. Inside was a piece of heavy white paper on which were pasted some individual letters cut out of magazines. The letters were MURDERER. They were very large and very colourful, clearly cut out with loving care from a variety of magazines. They'd been placed not in a straight line but unevenly, as if they were dancing. The effect was rather artistic. I stood on tiptoe and propped it up on the shelf which had formerly contained my collection of alabaster jars.

Beattie gave me a reproachful look. 'Put it in the fireplace, Hollyhock.'

I shook my head.

After four or five of the jars had been broken by various children I'd given the rest to one of Camille's CND jumble sales. I'd never got around to taking down the shelf. Now I looked around and saw how bare the room was. Andrew had taken away those pieces of furniture that were obviously his. He'd also taken the television. I'd never replaced the record player Dominic destroyed and had, almost without noticing, given away most of my records. I also hadn't replaced the plants Zach had eaten. All that was left was the sofa, one chair, the oriental rug, and my grandfather clock, all of them as scuffed and tatty as the walls which, yes, I hadn't got around to repainting. The card was the one touch of colour in the whole room, the only thing that was bright and new and clean.

'Holly,' said Beattie, getting up and walking towards the shelf.

'Leave it,' I said.

Two days later I received through the post an envelope with a typewritten address and our town's postmark. It contained the local newspaper account of Dominic's death.

A week after that I received another, much fatter, envelope. This one contained several clippings, some from the national tabloids. It too had a local postmark and typewritten address. I compared them. They'd been done with different typewriters.

There were also, around that time, some heavy-breather phone calls. I don't know if there's any connection.

Barnaby was quite upset. He even offered to come and stay with me till it all blew over. Given his love of solitude, this was generosity of a very high order. I thanked him but said no. 'What's the danger?' I said. 'The only killer around here is me.'

The friends with whom I'd attended concerts and plays and worked on committees began to avoid me. Perhaps they thought I wished to be alone. Two of them suggested that I might be happier away from our insulated little town, starting a new life somewhere else, maybe even changing my name. After a while it seemed the only people I saw outside work were Barnaby and Alice and Diana and Camille. Then Camille left.

35

I forget whether it was the autumn or the early winter of 1982 that the women set up their peace camp at Greenham Common. What I do remember is that Camille wasn't one of the founders. This upset her. She liked to be in on the action. Heaven knows she had enough to do – CND was booming in a way it hadn't even in the early sixties. But there sat all those women, their numbers growing daily, engaged in something that was new and radical and exciting in a way that CND could never be. And Camille wasn't one of them. The problem, of course, was Emma.

Now twelve, Emma looked almost exactly like Camille at that age – and, for that matter, like Camille's mother before her: all three of them small and vivacious and popular and sufficiently bright to charm teachers while not antagonizing their peers. Emma loved school. When Camille, in a conspiratorial manner designed to win over her daughter, proposed a few weeks' truancy from school, Emma was horrified. They had a row (Emma had also inherited her mother's temper) and the subject was dropped. That evening Camille came to see me. Would I mind terribly? Just for a few weeks?

I, who had killed off her only son a few months before, was now being entrusted with her only daughter.

Emma and I had never got on very well, but she tolerated the temporary move because I lived within walking distance of her school and most of her friends. This facilitated her very active social life. I, for my part, tolerated the move because it symbolized Camille's forgiveness.

Things went pretty well at first. The boxroom made a reasonable single bedroom – though, even with half the books and bookcases (Andrew's) removed, there was still no room for a desk. At any rate, I'd sold mine years before. That meant Emma had to do her homework either at the kitchen table or on the living room sofa – usually the latter because that room was warmest.

The hassles started when I found myself playing the heavy: if you can't be home at such-and-such a time, at least phone and tell me where you are. That kind of thing. It's not surprising that I felt more than usually anxious. Not only did Camille trust me, but Mummy depended on me to look after her sole surviving grandchild.

Away from the social milieu in which she thrived, Emma was a quiet child, sullen and self-possessed. We didn't talk much. My friendly queries ('Did you have a good day at school?') were seen as spying. We lapsed into a relationship much like an old stale marriage, eating our meals together in silence, scarcely noticing each other's presence. So I was surprised when, one night in December, she initiated a conversation.

We were both working in the living room – she on the sofa and me in the chair. (The cuts in public spending were hurting, and I had to bring a lot of work home just to keep up.) Emma was writing a composition or something for school. After a while, I noticed her pen had stopped. I looked up. She was staring self-consciously at the piece of white pasteboard which declared her aunt a murderer.

'Did Grandma give you that?' she said.

'Why would she do such a thing? No, it was anonymous. Someone put it through the letterbox the day of Dominic's funeral.'

Emma nodded sagely and returned to her writing. What timing! Perhaps she'll become an actress.

I waited. She waited too. She was waiting for me to feed her the cue she'd set up. Finally I could wait no longer. 'What made you say that?' I asked.

'Oh. Just that Grandma said you killed Dominic because you were jealous because you don't have any children of your own.'

I felt I'd been kicked in the stomach. That I was in some way responsible for Dominic's death I accepted. That anyone could think me a jealous aunt committing a deliberate act of murder was quite another matter. Had my mother really said such a thing? I tried to think how to answer without slander – family diplomacy's a tricky business. 'I think perhaps you misunderstood,' I tried.

A mistake. Children are sensitive to aspersions on their understanding.

She smiled coolly. 'I don't think so.' And went back to her writing.

I played the next move better, i.e. I said nothing and went back to my own work. Fortunately, it was fairly mechanical and didn't require much concentration. We worked in silence for a while with only the ticking clock for company. Then I heard a voice as if from a distance.

'I know you don't like me.'

She seemed to be talking to herself. I didn't know what to say. As usual in such situations, I uttered the first banality that came to mind. 'Nonsense. Of course I like you.'

'That's all right,' she said. 'Mummy doesn't like me either.'

'That's ridiculous. Of course she likes you.'

'Daddy left because he didn't like me.'

'Your father left because he was enticed away by another woman – the same one, I might add, that enticed my own husband away. You had nothing to do with it.'

'Uncle Andrew left because you're old and because you wouldn't have children.'

I wondered if I'd ever behaved like this with Beattie. If so, her forgiveness was truly a marvel. Then I wondered if I would ever come to like Emma as Beattie came to like me. Right now it seemed improbable.

'Have you finished your homework?' I said.

Very slowly she tore some sheets of paper into small pieces and tossed them at the fireplace. They caught before tumbling out onto the oriental rug. The rug began to smoulder. I stepped on it till the smoke disappeared. I was tired of playing warder. If she'd really destroyed her homework, that was her problem.

The grandfather clock whirred and struck ten. Emma's bedtime, but I wasn't going to remind her. These were pretty adult things she'd been saying. Let her act like an adult and go to bed when she chose.

'I'm making a hot chocolate,' I said. 'Do you want one?'

'Yes, please.'

I made the hot chocolates. It was a relief to clatter around the kitchen. I thought about Dominic, reduced to a pile of ashes which Camille had scattered at Ryegill. If one of them had to die, why did it have to be Dominic?

I brought Emma her drink. As I leaned over the back of the sofa to put it down on the arm, I saw the light gleaming off her long brown hair and the crooked parting in the middle. The sight of that fragile bit of human skull was too much, and I felt ashamed of my thoughts. One could hardly blame Emma for being a 'problem child', shuttled around between a too-busy mother and philandering father and uncaring aunt. How lucky I'd been with Daddy and Beattie. Even Mummy, busy with her flowers, had had time for me. I wished I could love Emma, or even just say something nice that would please her and make her feel like a valid human being. But everything I said she twisted against me. The best I could do was be an unobtrusive background during the little time remaining of my guardianship.

She raised the mug of chocolate, then frowned and sniffed at it. I didn't pay much attention. It was a new brand and perhaps smelled different. I took a sip of my chocolate and returned to my work. I didn't get very far. I could feel her eyes on me and looked up to intercept a suspicious look. Almost immediately it disappeared and she smiled.

'Would you mind if we changed mugs?' she asked. 'Mine has a crack.'

'Does it?' I looked. There was indeed a hairline crack, though smaller than the one on mine. Still, if it pleased her. I handed mine over and took hers in exchange.

I went back to my work again. Suddenly I realized what she was getting at. I looked at the card on the shelf and then at Emma. Why hadn't I taken the card down? Beattie was right: I was playing the martyr, accepting a guilt that didn't belong to me.

'Emma,' I said. 'You were there. On the pier. You know exactly what happened.'

'I don't know what you're talking about,' she said.

'Yes you do. You've spent the last hour or so accusing me in various oblique ways of murdering your brother. You were there. You know what happened. I admit a certain degree of responsibility. I should have stopped the two of you running around like that. But you were running, too. You were older than him. You should have known better than egg him on like that. If anyone's—'

I stopped, hoping I'd stopped soon enough.

The clock struck quarter past ten. Emma got up and drank the rest of her chocolate. I thought she was going to bed. I tried to think of something pleasant to say ('Never go to bed on a quarrel,' said Mummy). Then I noticed she was walking not to the stairs but to the grandfather clock in the corner. It was one of those glass-fronted ones with all the mechanism exposed. Emma stood contemplating it a moment. Then she swung back her leg and kicked in the glass.

36

When the Greenham women announced their intention to stay right through Christmas the country was stunned. An Indian Summer autumn in the open is one thing; sleeping bags in the snow is another. It was then that people began taking the women seriously.

No one was more stunned than Mummy, but she saved her real shock horror for Emma's announcement that she was going to join her mother at the camp for Christmas. A row followed, but Emma, like her mother and like her mother's mother before her, always got her way. Off she went, leaving Mummy with a big turkey and no family.

Relations between us had deteriorated so badly I thought it tactful to wait for an invitation. I hoped it wouldn't come. Beattie had asked me to spend Christmas with her and I would have really liked that. But the invitation came. Mummy also invited Beattie but Beattie declined. 'Pressure of work,' she said. (Coward.)

It was even more awful than the previous Christmas. Just the two of us bickering over a turkey big enough to feed the whole of Greenham Common. I envied Camille and Emma. Rather the honest cold of the weather than the chill that surrounded Mummy and me like a couple of frozen haloes.

Emma did indeed have a great time at Greenham. All the women treated her like the adult she perceived herself to be. When the holiday finished and the time came for her to return to her dreary old aunt, she refused. More rows. At last a compromise: Emma would return to school but stay with her best friend. What the best friend's parents thought of this is not known, but with Camille and Emma and the friend all in favour, I suppose they didn't have much choice.

I turned forty that Christmas.

37

A foggy late-autumn day. Earlier the sun was out, a summer-weakened remnant which had to work hard to pierce the mist. Still, it made it, and the glistening leaves of my evergreen namesake shone out smugly among its leafless companions. Now the sun's gone and the earth is turned grey and mysterious. The bare trees have come into their own, posing grandly in their skeletons. I watch an ancient beech on the squire's boundary, try to catch the moment its delicate twigs merge into the mist and vanish. Its elegance shames the fussy old holly. A wind gets up. The holly sees its chance and tries to shake off its tedious leaves. They rattle furiously while the beech's limbs dance a pretty minuet. I don't think it means to mock.

38

I want to make this brief. There's been enough about death. This is, I hope, the last one I'll have to record.

On Valentine's Day 1983 Beattie died. Despite her preparations it caught her out; she died (peacefully, as they say – I hope it's true) in her sleep of ordinary heart failure. I like to think she was dreaming of her Utopia in which the human race evolved to the point of being able to recognize the strange beauty and freedom of choice. If she had a tombstone, I would engrave on it a single word:

CHOOSE

I'll spare the details of my grief. The worst of it lasted a month. This (I read recently) is normal; the body is programmed to tolerate a month's worth of misery. After that, recovery begins or the body dies.

The strange thing about Beattie's death was the lack of guilt. If I hadn't been a good daughter to Daddy or a good aunt to Dominic, at least I'd been a good niece to Beattie. I searched my conscience for self-recrimination and found none.

After the first terrible month, I began to see Beattie. These were not hallucinations but deliberate attempts to keep her alive in my mind. Oddly enough, I saw her most in the garden, a place she intensely disapproved of.

'All this effort,' she sighed the last time she visited

me alive. It was sometime between Dominic's death and Greenham Common and she was sitting on a wooden seat by the magnolia watching me tidy up the garden.

'It's what I'm good at,' I said.

'You might be good at other things,' she said.

'Like having children?' A recent letter from Andrew had referred to my 'splendid hips, made for child-bearing, being wasted'. Beattie and I had laughed over it.

She wasn't laughing now. 'It's your wasted mind I worry about.'

'I use it at work.'

'Mechanical work.'

'And in the garden. Gardening requires a tremendous amount of thinking, you know.'

'To what end?'

'Don't be such a snob.' I wheeled the barrow a few yards farther down the path and continued extracting branches that had fallen onto the borders in the last high winds. One of them was a rowan with bright red berries. I had mixed feelings about rowans. Their premature berrying made August feel like autumn and that always depressed me a little, but their early leafing compensated and stayed the execution I sometimes threatened.

Beattie lit a cigarette and followed me. In a gesture of good will she plucked a branch from some veronicas and put it in the barrow. 'You have such a good mind, Holly.'

'Me and a few million others.'

'If only you weren't too lazy to use it.'

'Just smell this dianthus,' I said, picking one for her. 'It's called Loveliness. A bit like honeysuckle.'

She put it to her nose absentmindedly. 'You're quiet. You notice things and think about them in original ways.'

'Camille says I have a mind like a hamster's wheel.'

'Not always. Sometimes you think outside conventions.'

'Like?' We'd reached the boundary with the squire's land. I looked at the oak I'd planted to replace the one mangled by the deer. A few months later I would think about the deer again when Emma smashed my clock.

'Don't be so obtuse,' said Beattie.

I record these remarks not out of vanity but because, though I didn't know it at the time, they were the start of a campaign. It didn't end with her death either. The first time she visited me after she died, she came right out with it:

'Why don't you go back to university?'

What a peculiar question! 'What for?'

The reply was immediate. 'To read sociology and politics.'

I laughed. 'And who would teach me now that you're gone?'

The pause was slightly flustered – Beattie wasn't used to compliments. 'There are others.'

'But I'm not interested in sociology and politics.'

'That's why you should read them.'

I sighed and went back to the hedge. A rugosa was looking in a bad way. Should I prune right back or treat it gently? It's so hard imagining what it feels like to be a plant. I sank the secateurs into a branch.

'You're ignoring me,' she said.

'Beattie, what would I do with a degree in sociology and politics?'

'Research.'

'Into?' The branch was still green inside. I shouldn't have cut it.

'Hasn't it occurred to you that there's one minority that's never been researched?'

'I don't believe it.'

'A minority to which you belong and about which you've

already acquired a certain amount of empirical knowledge...'

The tutorial lead again.

'A minority which is penalized by society for making a choice which benefits society...'

I put the secateurs down. 'Beattie,' I said, 'I have no wish to do research on that or anything else. Is that clear?'

'Such a waste of a good mind,' she sighed.

'What about yours? You didn't have to smoke and drink so much. You didn't have to die so soon. You could still be here.'

There was a long pause. Then she said, very gently, 'Righteous indignation doesn't suit you, Holly.'

I burst into tears and fled to the house.

I didn't venture out for some time. When I did, it was to inspect what had been Andrew's vegetable patch. Alice and Diana no longer needed it – their own land was producing well by now. I'd never had such a large bare area to plan and was dizzy with choice.

'How about a commune?' she said.

She'd startled me, suddenly at my elbow.

'I was thinking of a herb garden,' I replied.

'You could move in with Barnaby – turn that monstrosity into a commune. Single adults only. Like-minded people. Set an example. Study-groups. Talks to local organizations, then—'

I stared at her. 'Barnaby??? A commune???'

She prodded a clod of earth with her sensible shoe. 'Hmmm. Perhaps not.'

I was clearing the patch of the remains of its previous existence. The soil was rich after years of manuring for vegetables. There was nothing that wouldn't grow there. I contemplated some aristocratic shrubs I'd envied for years and been unable to find room for.

'I have an idea,' she said.

She was leaning on the spade – not using it, just leaning.

'Yes?' I said.

'Adult literacy classes for immigrants. You could use the library, organize a group of volunteers. Do a little consciousness raising while you're at it.'

'Beattie,' I said.

'Yes?'

'There are no immigrants in this town.'

It was an ideal spot for a rockery, but the only rockeries I liked were large ones with running water and ferny areas tucked under big trees. That would take an acre at least. Besides, there was no running water.

'Stand for election to the local council. Shake up this place. Find out what or who it is that's keeping the immigrants out.'

'Beattie,' I said. 'Please. Just sit there. Just keep me company. Please?'

'Why not something really radical?' she said.

I was coming to the same conclusion. It seemed a shame to use the space for just more shrubs and small trees and herbaceous plants. What I wanted was something big and dramatic and startling, something utterly out of keeping with suburbia.

'Leave your job,' she went on, 'and join Greenham.'

'And what do I live on?'

'Others have done it.'

She was sitting with her back to a shrubby willow, its soft yellow catkins forming a giant halo around her whole body. She lit a cigarette.

'Do they allow smoking up there?' I asked.

'Very tolerant they are,' said Beattie. 'Free choice in everything.'

I laughed, but she wasn't so easily diverted.

'At least go for Easter,' she tried.

'It's swarming with kids now.'

'True, but you could—'

'Beattie,' I said, 'for someone so keen on choice you're very eager to impose your will on me.'

I had her there. She stood up and brushed some dead leaves off her skirt. She smiled. '*Touché.*'

But in death, as in life, she didn't give up easily.

'At least write to your MP,' she said.

'What about?'

'Anything. Cruise missiles. Immigration quotas. Unequal job opportunities in the north. Unequal NHS facilities for the childfree.'

I was digging a large pit in the centre of the patch. Very large. I peered at her through sweat that was running freely despite a cool March breeze. 'Beattie,' I said. 'Please? Just sit there and keep me company?'

The pit was finished. Beattie looked into it dubiously. Around it stood piles of fresh rich earth, waiting. She walked to the edge of the patch and stared at a clump of daffodils. She seemed a bit down. 'A little agit-prop graffiti?'

'Can you see me with a spray can?'

She shook her head sadly. 'What am I to do with you?'

'Stay and keep me company.'

On Easter weekend of 1983, three thousand Glaswegians lay on the streets with paper bags over their heads after an 'air raid' siren sounded.

At the other end of the country 70,000 people formed a human chain between Aldermaston and Greenham Common. Two of them were Camille and Emma. I felt terribly proud of them.

Over in Europe, Defence Secretary Michael Heseltine visited the Berlin Wall.

I planted a giant sequoia.

39

Things would have been easier if Andrew had left me alone; a neat clean break I could have got used to. In fact, he'd been writing to me for years.

It began shortly after he left his oboist and moved to London. The first letter was extraordinary. No mention of the oboist, or of children, or of the fact that he'd just chucked his wife and done a flit. The tone was that of two old lovers temporarily separated and anticipating their reunion.

'How should I answer it?' I asked Alice.

She was incredulous. 'You want to answer it?'

'Well, of course.' The thought of an unanswered letter was intolerable. I'm a neat person. I can't stand loose ends.

'Guarded but Friendly,' she advised at last.

I wrote. Two weeks later he wrote back. Pretty soon he was enclosing glossy brochures of 'family homes' in the stockbroker belt. Even on the prestige salary that went with his prestige job he couldn't afford such places. Sure enough, the next step was the Situations Vacant pages of the *TLS* with certain library jobs encircled in red.

'What do I do now?' I asked Alice.

She dumped the Situations Vacant and the brochures in the wastepaper basket. 'More Guarded, less Friendly,' she said.

Not so Andrew. His letters soon developed a pattern. The first part was a paeon to family life as exemplified by

Gillian and her four children. Given his open hostility to same whenever they'd dumped themselves on us, this was truly astonishing. I should say that by this time Des had gone and Andrew was *de facto* head of the family.

Diana summed up the situation. 'Before he owned one person; now he owns five. What power!'

'But she's his sister!'

'A slave is a slave.'

The second half was a paeon of praise to his mistress, i.e. me. I think I mentioned earlier that Andrew had changed my self-image from earth mother to odalisque. For this I was, and am, grateful. But now the two were merging. The image that rose from those letters was quite something. No doubt about it: I was the embodiment of the Eternal Feminine, the Mater Gloriosa, the Urweib.

I looked in the mirror and saw a dowdy librarian pushing forty. Who was he trying to kid?

'If he's so keen on having children,' said Alice, 'why doesn't he divorce you and remarry?'

Why indeed? Perhaps there's a dearth of Urweibs in Sussex. I thought about Gillian and Andrew and me. A curious trio we made – all of us large, fleshy, voluptuous in appearance. A sinister idea crept into my mind. Had Andrew married me because I was the nearest thing to his sister? They were, after all, twins. Twins traditionally enjoy a special closeness. Perhaps he'd been reluctant to relinquish this and chosen me as a near substitute.

I couldn't match their respectability though. In middle age the inherent conservatism of their race was taking over. Andrew looked like a bright well-fed backbencher waiting his turn. (He came to both Daddy's and Dominic's funerals. 'So considerate,' murmured Mrs Trevelyan after the latter.) Soon Gillian would start wearing hats.

The respectability gap between Andrew and me widened

further after these deaths. I tried not to notice all the little signs that signified my descent. Alice and Diana and Barnaby tried, too, but it was obvious that they heard things. Finally I couldn't stand it any longer. 'Tell me what they're saying,' I said.

They told me. I expect it was an expurgated version. Even so, it shocked. From being a minor pillar of the community I'd turned into an unnatural wife, a heartless daughter and a vindictive aunt. The company I kept probably didn't help, as my ravens were no doubt aware: two lesbians and a hermit.

I wasn't too worried. I loved my funny friends, and if my house had been ravaged by other people's children, it was still a roof over my head and had the garden as compensation. I was also financially secure. The only person above me was the County Librarian, and I was far too good at my job to sack because of some local talk.

None the less, the talk reached Andrew and the tone of his letters changed. The paeon of love became a shade condescending. Though veiled, the message was clear: Andrew in his magnanimity would rehabilitate me. When I failed to respond, an element of threat appeared. His generosity had a time limit. At forty I would become (a) invisible; and (b) too old for motherhood. Tick tick.

On my fortieth birthday he wrote to me and asked for a divorce. I pictured him clearing a space in the debris of turkey and paper hats. 'Dear Madam,' though of course he didn't use those words.

I ignored the letter, and the next, and the next. For the first time in my life I learned the power of inertia.

Then Beattie died and I hardly noticed the letters. Perhaps they stopped for a while, I don't remember.

Sometime in the late spring or early summer of 1983 I

173

received another letter stating Andrew's desire for a divorce. This one was from his solicitor, so I couldn't ignore it. After an exchange of several letters, Andrew's position emerged as follows:

He wanted a divorce and half of the property which was in our joint names. This, he made clear, showed considerable generosity on his part, given that I was both an unnatural wife and an adulteress (Barnaby was mentioned) and had moreover 'led him on' with hopes of reconciliation for the five years since our 'separation' (the oboist, but she wasn't mentioned).

I contemplated the contestants that were emerging:

Andrew, who, upset by his wife refusing to have children, commits a minor indiscretion and then, quite naturally, accepts an offer of promotion and moves south where he has since lived a respectable and blameless life with his sister and her four children, taking up the burden of caring for them after desertion by husband and father.

Holly, who denies her husband children, refuses to mourn her father's death, is implicated in the death of her nephew, cares only for her garden, and chooses as her best friends two lesbians and as her lover an eccentric manual labourer.

Given such damning evidence, Andrew could ignore Beattie's downpayment on the mortgage and the five years I'd been financing the mortgage alone.

Fifty-fifty.

There were two ways to split the property. Either we sell it and share the profit. Or we have it valued by a mutually-agreed estate agent and I pay Andrew half the valuation and put the remainder of the mortgage in my name alone. As I had no wish to leave, I chose the latter.

The results made me reel. In the seventeen years I'd lived here the whole terrace had gone up-market. This I knew. What I didn't know was the site of my garden – two unused building plots – would revert in the valuation to building plots. True, they didn't have planning permission. But the town was eager to expand in that direction, and permission was virtually certain. I was, to use a cliché, sitting on a gold mine.

Fat help it was to me. I might be able to finance the mortgage, but no way could I do so *and* find a lump sum of such magnitude to pay off Andrew.

I ran through the possibilities.

I could apply for planning permission and sell off the two plots. That would give me just about enough to pay Andrew and leave me with a house and a skinny little strip of garden out the back.

Eden gone. What was the point of staying?

Or Barnaby could sell his house, move in with me, and pay off Andrew. It was too much to ask of anyone. He might do it out of solidarity and, well, yes, love. But he'd hate it here. Barnaby without his hermit's retreat was like my house without its garden. What was the point of that either?

The third possibility was to give up and sell. I could always move to a flat or some other house with a pocket-handkerchief garden. 'Coward,' whispered the monkey who took up residence on my shoulder at about this time.

Give up altogether and go back to Andrew? I scarcely finished the thought before rejecting it. Anyway, I was past child-bearing age, invisible, as dead to him as Beattie was to—

Beattie. Beattie's will.

40

I now think it extraordinary that it took me so long to think of Beattie's will. Now, however, I went straight into action. The first step was to phone Mummy.

'Has Beattie's estate been settled yet?' I asked. (There seemed no virtue in being delicate about it.)

There was a pause. 'I don't believe so,' she replied. The phrase was fractionally out of character, as was the pause.

'Why not?' I asked.

Another pause. 'These things take time.'

'Five months?' I said.

'The law is a very complicated organism.' That was more characteristic.

'Can anything be done to speed things up?' I asked. 'I need the money fast.'

A long pause this time. Then, 'What money?'

'The money she left me,' I said.

I felt so impatient I almost missed the thin tone of her next remark: 'What makes you think she left you any money?'

It was I who paused this time. Thank God I did, and that some instinct made me cautious. 'She only had two nieces,' I said. 'It's only natural that she would leave something to us.' Note the *us*. Did I suspect already?

'I don't know anything about that,' she said.

The same instinct made me drop the subject. Even while chatting about other things, my mind was working. The next day was my day off. I'd planned to repair the edging to the frog pond but that could wait and so could the weeding. As Mummy talked on and on about the Potters and other neighbours I scarcely remembered, I became more certain that something was up. What, I didn't know, but I did know I'd have to be cunning.

I hardly slept that night and set off early the next morning. I reached London before ten. Mummy was in the garden. I need hardly say she was surprised to see me – and perhaps a little nervous? Even so, my misgivings remained unfocused. In the car I'd prepared an opening move designed to throw the suspicion elsewhere. That way I might catch her off-guard and startle something out of her. I didn't have a proper plan – I just felt that an indirect approach was more likely to work.

'Beattie's solicitor is a crook,' I said, 'and I mean to expose him.' I watched her face carefully and saw the alarm I expected.

'Good heavens,' she said faintly. Then she turned and continued hoeing beneath the roses. That meant I couldn't see her face, which is probably what she intended.

I'd read somewhere that the best way of eliciting confessions was silence. The suspect can't bear silence and has to break it. In so doing, he/she often reveals something. So I waited.

It was July, the middle of another drought. The sun was already hot and brought beads of sweat out on my forehead. I wiped them off, just in case she turned around and interpreted them as nerves, which perhaps they were.

She stopped hoeing and spoke. 'Do you think that's wise?'

'Why?' I asked.

'Well, you know; the law is so powerful. They don't like being interfered with.'

'Exactly,' I said. 'They don't like crooked solicitors. They're pretty quick to spot them, too.' I don't know if that's true. Much of what I said that morning was bluff.

'Why should he be crooked?' she asked. 'What does he stand to gain?'

'A rake-off?' I suggested, using a term I vaguely remembered from detective films.

'I don't understand,' she said.

'I think you do,' I said quietly. It embarrassed me to be staging a B-film scene, but it was the only way I could think of.

She went back to her hoeing. She was hoeing much too deeply, threatening the superficial roots. Very suspicious in such an experienced gardener, thought Detective Superintendent Holly.

'There's nothing crooked about it,' said Mummy. 'I'm her next of kin. It's always the next of kin who inherits.'

'Not if there's a will,' I said.

'There was no will,' she said.

'There was a will,' I said. 'And that's why I have an appointment with a probate lawyer today.' It was the first of several lies I'd prepared. Mummy was so ignorant of the law that I knew I could get away with anything.

She turned pale. She actually turned pale, just like in the books. 'You can't do that,' she said.

'Why not?' I said. 'I have proof.'

By now she was as white as the Blanc Double de Coubert she'd just stopped torturing with her hoe. 'Now that you mention it, he did say something about a will,' she said. 'Yes, now I remember. He said there *had* been a will. Yes, that's right, now I remember. She'd taken it home to change it and I guess she changed her mind or something and decided not to have one after all.'

'The solicitor knew what was in that will,' I said.

'Did he?'

'He drew it up. It was originally in his office, remember?'

'Yes, of course. Yes, he did say something, a big list of bits and pieces or something. It's a pity about that, but—' She smiled brightly. 'Perhaps we can put things right? I mean, you might be able to guess which bits were meant for which person and then I could send the things. Wouldn't that be a good idea!'

'I can do more than guess,' I said. Then I took a deep breath and uttered my second and most dangerous lie. 'I have the will.'

Shock, horror, confusion. I had no idea she would be so transparent. 'That's impossible,' she said.

'Why?'

'There was only one,' she said.

'No, there wasn't. Beattie xeroxed it for me. She gave me a copy.' The third lie. I hoped she wouldn't query such odd behaviour. Why, after all, should Beattie give me a copy? It would make more sense to give her literary executor a copy. Ah, must remember that. The threat of a *second* xerox.

'A xerox isn't the same,' she said. 'It's not legal.'

'Probably not,' I admitted. 'But it's pretty damning evidence.' I looked at my watch, hoping she would connect the gesture with my 'appointment'.

'It's probably out of date,' she said.

'Perhaps. What was the date of the one you saw?'

'I don't remember.'

Did she realize what she'd just said? Up till then I'd been guessing. I spoke quickly to prevent her from thinking. 'Did he give you his key or did you go there together?'

'Of course he didn't. I wasn't there. He opened it himself. I don't know when.'

Second slip. 'It' could only refer to the safe, which hadn't been mentioned and which she shouldn't know anything about.

'What else was in it?' I asked.

'Just some boring old papers,' she said. 'They went to the university.'

'Went?'

She looked at me as if I were a cretin. 'They went to the university,' she repeated. 'I gave them away. What use were they to me?'

Then the estate *had* been settled. 'What have you done with your money?' I asked.

'Put it away for my grandchildren.'

I ignored the plural. 'And the pills?'

'Flushed them down the lavatory! Filthy obscene things! Your aunt was depraved, Holly. I hate to say it of my own sister but she was and it's only by the grace of God that she was prevented from using those horrible things.' She turned on me with unmistakable triumph. 'So you can do what you like with your xerox or whatever because your aunt was insane when she made that will and it doesn't count because anyone who even contemplates suicide is insane and I have proof of it!'

I closed my eyes. I couldn't believe my luck. When I opened them, she was still gloating. She still hadn't realized. 'Mother,' I said, 'do you realize what you've just said? About those pills that are supposed to prove Beattie's insanity and which, at any rate, you flushed down the toilet, thus destroying your "proof"? Those pills, Mother: you got them out of Beattie's safe. You broke into Beattie's safe before the solicitor got there and you destroyed the pills. And when you saw her will and saw that she'd left virtually everything to me, you destroyed that, too. That is a very serious criminal offence.'

Mr Potter came out into his garden next door and waved to us. I waved back cheerfully. Mummy dropped her hoe and walked quickly into the house. I followed her. She sat down by the dead fireplace in front of which she'd placed an arrangement of dried flowers and grasses.

'Beattie was a selfish old spinster,' she said savagely.
'They always are. They don't know the first thing about
Christian humility and self-sacrifice. Who do they have to
sacrifice themselves to? They live their whole lives for
themselves and then when they die they just keep on being
selfish.' She gave me a look of pure hatred. 'Yes, I saw her
will. And when I saw how selfish she'd been in it, I destroyed
it. You think I did it because I wanted the money. Well,
you're wrong. I'm putting most of the money in trust for
Emma, and the rest of it is going on her education. Emma
is going to a public school – this year, if I can arrange it in
time.'

I had anticipated getting a confession out of her. What I
hadn't anticipated was the cornered animal turning vicious.
I didn't know how to respond. 'Does Camille know this?' I
asked.

'None of your business.'

'Does she know about the will?'

'You can do what you like with your xerox. Xeroxes
aren't the same, and anyway it's all over. The estate is
settled.'

'I can contest it,' I said. The fourth lie. I didn't even
have a xerox.

She smiled. 'And how much will that cost you?'

'Maybe I'm willing to do it for Beattie's sake? To defend
her wishes? As a matter of principle?'

'Then I'll fight you with my principles.'

'Which are?'

'You killed Dominic and now you're trying to cheat
Emma. That poor child, dragged into that disgusting
women's camp, I don't know what Camille can be thinking
of, she's as bad as you are. I don't know what I've done to
deserve two such terrible children but I do know one thing
and that's that Emma isn't going to end up like either of
you. I may have failed with you two, but I'm not going to

fail Emma. I'm all she has now what with a lunatic mother and a heartless monster for an aunt and her father leaving like that and I intend to make sure she grows up into a decent normal woman and I'll spend every penny I have fighting you if you try to prevent me because a human soul like that is worth everything if you weren't such a selfish monster like your aunt that you can't even see a simple truth like that—'

41

I break off to spare my mother what little dignity she has left.

Driving back, I forced myself to think of other things. I recited nursery rhymes, I sang to myself, anything to keep my mind off that gruesome scene. Even so, I was shaking so much I shouldn't have been driving at all.

When I got back I felt a great need to tell someone, to share my indignation and fury. But it seemed unfair to use Alice in that way (Mummy was, after all, her aunt), and Barnaby had such a horror of emotional scenes that I decided to spare him, too.

So I brooded and raged and crashed about the house alone all evening. I don't know what infuriated me more: being cheated out of the money, or the outrage committed against Beattie's wishes. I still wonder if I should have at least made an effort and gone to Beattie's solicitor. But what would I have said? My only evidence was verbal. All I could say was that I'd seen her will and that my mother had confessed privately to me. Even the best intentioned solicitor couldn't do much with that. And what about the picture which my mother painted of me and which would be dragged through whatever courts were involved in such things? My public image was pretty low by now, and there would be added to it the element of rapacious aunt trying to diddle her only niece out of a good education. I wondered in passing how Camille would react when Mummy swooped and deposited Emma in a public school of all things. I also wondered what she'd think if she knew the money for it had been stolen from me. The monkey on my shoulder made an unprintable reply. I agreed. Never had the world looked so black. Everyone in it – myself included – seemed foul and rotten and stinking with a stench that rose straight up to heaven, and in a moment of suffocation in which I thought my lungs would burst, I raged through the back door and into the garden.

I'd almost forgotten the garden. My garden, sacrificed to my mother's crime. The one pure place, my sanctuary, symbol of what we'd all lost.

The roses were blooming. I walked down the hedge in the dark, inhaling deeply, willing them to comfort me. I stopped by a sweet briar and sniffed at its leaves. It helped, a little. There are no miracles even in Eden, but bit by bit my garden would work the modest magic I'd relied on so long. 'It's like a drug, your garden,' Beattie once said. I'd been indignant. What about her whisky and cigarettes? We all had our drugs. So what?

I sat down by the magnolia where I'd last seen her. Even Beattie wasn't safe from the monkey. 'Do you really think she cares? – that you'll lose your garden because you've lost her money?'

'Shut up,' I told it. 'That isn't the point.'

The monkey shrugged.

And then – strange juxtaposition – as the monkey faded from sight I had the first cheering thought for days. '*Choose,*' *said Beattie.* My mother had chosen – my money rather than me. In so doing, she had unintentionally released me. She had one daughter now. Camille, not I, would tend her old age – Camille and my money. I was free.

42

It was rather a lonely summer. The marvellous weather (three months of sun and no rain) meant Barnaby was once again working flat out. By now he'd started the first of his small-is-beautiful houses. His clients (an academic couple forced into 'early retirement' by the government) were plagued by other people's yapping dogs and had bought an isolated patch of land to get some peace and quiet. On this land was a tiny derelict outbarn with planning permission. They had quite a job scrapping the old plans and getting the council to accept Barnaby's, but they managed it. I visited the site two or three times. On one occasion all five of us worked together, myself and the clients acting as navvies to Barnaby and his mate, but I didn't feel I should go there too often. Still, Barnaby was so happy I didn't mind.

When the school holidays started, Emma went back to Greenham Common, this time escorted by Diana. They both planned to spend the whole summer. Alice would have, too, but she only had four weeks' holiday. I wished I could bend the rules for her, but it was out of the question and she understood. We joked about being grass widows.

In the middle of July came the scene with my mother.

At the beginning of August, Alice took her four weeks and went off to Greenham.

She returned alone. Emma, she reported, was looking

forward to boarding school. Camille had made a scene about élitist capitalist bourgeois conspiracies and had then given in. The chosen school was single-sex and that evidently cancelled out everything else.

'And Diana?' I asked.

'She's staying at Greenham.'

'But—'

'Diana and Camille are lovers,' said Alice, and burst into tears.

Alice gave a month's notice to leave her job. I wanted to dissuade her but felt constrained by my own sense of guilt. It was, after all, my sister who had lured Diana away. Not that Alice held it against me. During that month we became quite close. I hadn't realized till then just how much I valued her, both as an employee and a friend. She was irreplaceable.

'Where will you go?' I asked.

'To the States.'

I didn't inquire further.

43

Diana came back at the end of September to transfer her belongings to Ryegill. The house next door was already pretty bare; Alice had sent two trunksful of stuff to the States and was spending her last few days with me. I remembered the first time she'd occupied the spare room, with Zach all those years ago. I couldn't believe so much had happened since.

Diana didn't come back alone. Camille was with her, resplendent in dungarees and a pair of those little earrings in the shape of the female symbol which Diana had given her. I felt terribly sorry for Alice. Diana had been the great love of her life. But, as a lesbian, she disapproved of 'owning' people, and she greeted the new couple with as much solidarity and affection as she could manage.

There was a third member of the entourage: a baby. I viewed it warily. Diana and Camille misunderstood.

'No,' Camille laughed, 'she isn't ours.'

'Yes, she is, legally she's ours,' said Diana, and produced from her back pocket an extraordinary document.

I put on my glasses and read.

'I, _____ _____, resident of the Women's Peace Camp, Greenham Common, Berkshire, do hereby record the birth of my baby, Peace, born at the above address on the Second of September, Nineteen Hundred and Eighty-Three. Peace was conceived in war, the result of a rape by my former husband. For this reason I do not feel I can be a proper and loving mother to her and I do hereby relinquish all rights to her. In the hopes that Peace may triumph over War, I entrust the sole guardianship and legal responsibility for this baby to my two sisters recorded below.'

There followed Camille and Diana's names with two addresses each – Greenham Common and Ryegill. The document ended with the signatures of two witnesses and the date.

'I don't think it's legal,' I said. 'What about the father?'

Rude remarks from the two guardians.

'That may well be,' I said, 'but I still think he has legal rights.'

'How will they find him?' Diana laughed.

It was true. Nowhere was he named, and Diana further told me that the mother had used her maiden name. Even so, he could no doubt be traced.

'Let him try,' said Diana.

I shrugged. 'It's your business,' I said. And we went into the kitchen to eat.

It was a full house that night. I'd asked Barnaby over for dinner and saw no reason why I should retract the invitation to spare Diana's sensibilities. In a few days we were off to Germany for a week, our departure timed to coincide with Alice's so we could drive her to the airport. There were some architectural developments Barnaby wanted to see in Germany and he was looking forward to the trip at least as much as I was.

Perhaps that's what gave a holiday atmosphere to the evening. Without it we would have been in a right mess. The cross-relationships between the five of us (Peace didn't count) were potentially explosive. Once or twice I looked at Camille and thought, 'Thief.' But how could I blame her? She didn't know that Mummy's beneficence was a legacy stolen from me. I still hadn't told her, nor Alice, nor Barnaby.

I give Alice much of the credit for that amiable evening, but even she couldn't prevent the scene that ruined its end.

We'd finished dinner and gone into the living room where I had a nice fire going against the rainy autumn night. There was so little furniture left that some of us sat on the floor, but that created an even cosier atmosphere. I don't remember much of what we talked about over our coffee and sloe gin. After all, we didn't have much in common. My mind kept wandering, lured into memories by various sights (the space in the corner where my grandfather clock had been; the sloe gin we'd drunk that evening with Andrew and Beattie and me; Sara's coal smear on the one remaining chair). Even the five of us – the last time we'd been together was the day of the spud harvest when Barnaby repaired the downspout and Camille announced her resignation. Everywhere I looked, memories, and the monkey on my shoulder making its usual remarks.

Peace coughed. Her new parents went over to her basket and had a look. The monkey commented on what a loving father Diana was for someone who detested patriarchy. I told it to shut up.

'Do you think she's all right?' said Diana anxiously.

'Probably getting a cold,' said Camille.

'I'm not surprised,' I said. 'It must be freezing down there.'

'Don't you have any heat in your tent?' said Alice.

No, no heat.

'You'll have the NSPCC on you,' said Alice.

Barnaby was keeping very quiet. He later said he knew what was coming, but I think that was hindsight.

'I know,' said Camille. 'The other women are pretty nervous about it. Bad for our image.'

Barnaby tells me the two women exchanged a look at this

point. I was gazing into the fire and feeling grateful for the warmth that would be denied poor Peace when the entourage departed for Greenham – they were leaving the same day as the rest of us.

'Actually,' said Camille, 'we're not sure it's a good idea to take her back there.'

'Two women more or less won't make much difference,' I said.

There was a little pause before Diana spoke. 'Camille and I have to go back. We belong there.'

'It would appear there's a conflict of interest,' said Alice.

'Not if Holly looks after Peace.'

'WHAT???'

'Just for a few weeks, Holly,' said Camille.

'Our source in Whitehall tells us the showdown's coming any day now,' Diana added. 'After that we can all go home.'

'After what?' I said.

'After we prevent the missiles from coming,' said Camille impatiently.

'Are you out of your minds?' I said. 'Look, I admit that as a gesture Greenham Common is hot stuff, but no way are you going to prevent those missiles from coming. No way.'

Diana looked at Camille. 'It's really heartening, the faith your sister has in us.'

'And while we're on the subject,' I said, 'may I just point out that some of us are getting fed up with all those nappies and junk you stick on the fence. Has it occurred to you that that is a profoundly anti-feminist gesture? That with all your talk about "Peace for our children" all you're doing is perpetuating the one thing that prevents change? "Peace for our children" indeed! How about peace for the rest of us!'

'And what are you doing for peace?' Camille demanded. 'Sitting on your fat arse in the library and raking in the shekels and shacking up with the enemy that made all those missiles in the first place!'

'I will not have Barnaby called the enemy in this house! He's doing more to change the world than the whole lot of you put together!'

'Building nice little houses for nice little bourgeois couples,' Diana sneered.

We were back on the patio sorting spuds, only this time there was no nice Holly to chirp, 'Tea?' and avert disaster. I had leapt into the offensive in a way that would have been unimaginable then. 'That's right!' I said. 'Nice little bourgeois couples and single people who are fed up to the teeth with being second-best in a world full of selfish parents like you!'

'SELFISH? ME?' screamed Camille. 'Jesus Christ, I like that! Do you have any idea what it's like down there? Freezing to death in those crummy tents and then the local yobbos come and drive their motorcycles into them and practically kill us and every day risking our lives and arrest and God knows what else so people like YOU can sit on your fat arses in the warmth and dispense Jane Austen like it was going to save the world or something!'

Yet again, guilt. Always she exposed the ugly side of me and destroyed my anger with guilt. What could I say? She'd given up her job, her husband, her family, a comfortable life, first for CND, then Greenham, all for the sake of peace, while I—

'You think it's some kind of Girl Scout picnic or something?' yelled Camille. 'You just come down and try it yourself! Have we once even criticized you? Even Alice had the decency to come during her holiday! What have you ever done for peace? A few weeks of your precious time, that's all we're asking! You can't even look after one little baby a few weeks for peace?'

'Babysitting for peace? I, Holly, am singlehandedly going

to conquer Armageddon with a few weeks of babysitting? Camille, be realistic! I don't even like kids!'

'You think I like sitting in that freezing tent and—'

'All right!' I yelled. '*After* Germany. *After* Germany I'll look after your brat, but *not before*! And be it on your head if she turns out a mess like Emma because I have said it before and I'll say it again *I do not like children* and I will make no effort whatsoever to hide that feeling from her or anyone else! You're not the only one who's come out of the closet!'

Camille looked at Diana. 'My sister is going on holiday,' she explained, though Diana knew perfectly well because we'd talked about it that very evening. 'My sister kindly requests Armageddon to wait till she and her lover return from their holiday.' Then, 'For Christ's sake, why can't you take her with you?'

'It's too late to get her a passport. Anyway—' I stopped. I'd been about to add that children had a habit of dying when they went on holiday with me, but—

'They don't need passports that young,' said Diana.

'Yes, they do.'

'Holly...'

It was Barnaby. The force of his voice, silent for much of the evening, was dramatic. We all turned towards him.

'Holly, we're not taking that child with us – with or without a passport.'

I nodded. As far as I was concerned, that settled it.

'But we're leaving next week!' cried Camille. 'There's no one else! You *have* to take her!'

'Holly,' said Barnaby. 'If that child goes, I don't.'

'Typical male,' muttered Diana. She glared at Barnaby. 'What you're saying is that Holly has to choose between big gorgeous you and saving the world, right?'

'I wouldn't put it that way,' he said, 'but yes. To choose.'

'I've chosen,' I said. I looked at Camille and Diana. 'You

don't *have* to go back to Greenham next week. You can delay it. And while we're away, I expect you to look for someone else to dump that baby on. All those women who say they absolutely adore children, all right? Try one of them.'

'But you promised!'

'I said I'd look after her *after* Germany, and if you hold me to it, I will. But if you have the slightest interest in her welfare you'll find someone who wants her. That's all I have to say.'

Camille and Diana left, taking the baby with them. The evening had gone sour, and Barnaby left soon after. Even Alice was subdued, and we didn't stay up much longer.

I should have guessed what would happen. All the signs were there.

Barnaby stayed here the night before we were due to leave so we could get an early start. Not early enough. Before any of us was up the doorbell rang. I went down in my dressing gown and opened the door. At my feet was the basket containing Peace. Camille's car was disappearing down the road.

'That baby or me,' said Barnaby.

'But what can I do?' I cried. 'Leave her to die on the doorstep?'

Alice caught her plane. Barnaby went to Germany alone. I was left holding the baby. Literally.

44

Barnaby's been back from Germany for some time now, but I haven't got in touch with him. I don't dare. I know I let him down. 'Choose,' he said. 'Choose,' said Beattie.

'Camille didn't,' I say. 'She's had children *and* done something with her life.'

'One or other will suffer,' says Beattie.

'Dominic has.'

But choice, it seems, is one-way. 'All I wanted,' I tell my winter-bare magnolia, 'was the same respect and benefits for my choice as parents are given for theirs.'

'All you wanted,' she retorts, 'was to vegetate your life away in this garden. You got your wish.'

'Don't be hard on me, Beattie.'

She smiles, and I fancy I feel a faint pat on the head. 'Then do something. Now,' she says.

Peace cries from within the house and I picture her that day in her basket on the doorstep. 'What choice did I have?' But I did have a choice, and I failed. I can blame the exploitative parents as much as I like, but I helped them exploit me. If I hadn't been so 'nice' for so long, they wouldn't have battened on my life like so many blood-suckers. What good's an occasional protest? My character is set.

Beattie frowns.

She's right. I'm just making excuses for myself. There must be something I can do.

I've done something. I've taken Peace to Mrs Sproat. Yes, of course I'm the one who pays her. It doesn't matter. Money's not much use to me now – the amount I need to save my garden is utterly beyond possibility.

I've done something else: I've put my house up for sale. Beattie is amazed. 'The garden, too?' she says.

I've refused to give the estate agent a key, so all applicants are shown around by me personally. Because I'm not going to sell this place to just anyone. Here's my opening gambit:

'I'm afraid it's rather a death trap for children.' Then I show them all the hazards and watch their faces carefully.

Another trick. I mention the likelihood of planning permission for the two plots. Again, I watch their faces. At the first sign of greed, I tell them about the woodworm. Then I ask, very innocently, if they know the signs of the death watch beetle.

And another. I show them the boxroom. 'A nice nursery,' I suggest. A coy glance or a slight blush and I mention the subsidence.

All lies, of course. The house is the soundest I know. Barnaby would be furious if he knew my slander. The estate agent *is* furious. What can he do? What can Andrew do? Give up his job and come up here to sell it himself? Inertia. I wait.

45

14th November 1983. The first cruise missiles are airlifted into Greenham Common. Poor Camille. A whole year wasted. I wait for her to come back and claim Peace.

11th December 1983. The first snow of the year, only a light dusting but how lovely the garden looks.

Showed another couple around. Told them planning permission was unlikely. Their faces fell. I showed them the door.

Camille hasn't come back. They're staying to prevent the missiles from becoming operational.

25th December 1983. Turned forty-one. Mummy invited me for Christmas. I couldn't believe it. I asked her who she was stealing her turkey from and she hung up.

1st January 1984. The first cruise missiles made operational. Peace awaits her 'parents'.

2nd January 1984. Interview on the radio with one of the Greenham women. She says they'll never give up as long as a single missile remains at Greenham Common.

6th January 1984. Took a day off work, drove Peace to a children's home, and officially put her in care. They were very reluctant at first (I explained everything) but agreed that if the convoluted legalities could be sorted out, there might even be a possibility of adoption. If so, Peace would be snapped up. Seems they have an enormous waiting list of couples desperate to own good-quality babies.

Why didn't I think of it sooner?

13th January 1984. Employed another builder to repair gale-damaged roof. Odd and very sad to see someone else up there.

14th January 1984. Barnaby came around, furious that someone had tampered with 'his' roof. He seemed unaware of the three month silence. Made lunch for him.

21st January 1984. So much snow! Normally I love it but right now I wish it would go away. Another couple's coming tomorrow – weather willing – and I like the sound of them. They seem to know the place already. They also said something about having 'talked to _____' (the squire), though what he has to do with it I can't imagine.

22nd January 1984. I'm so excited I can hardly think! They came despite the snow and made no attempt to hide their enthusiasm. We spent about two minutes on the house (they passed all my tests) and the rest in the garden. They loved it, but that's only the beginning. They've both been to horticultural college and for years their dream has been to start a nursery of their own. The problem, of course, was money, but then an aunt died (Beattie!) and left them everything. Further, the squire's willing to give them an extremely long lease on an acre of land across the lane. They have friends in town and know there's no nursery for miles around. I can hardly believe it! She was wearing one of those old badges that says MAKE LOVE NOT BABIES. Should I lower the price? Yes!

46

This evening after dinner I put on the back light and went out into the garden to say goodbye. I won't be leaving for a while yet, but it seemed the right moment.

I hardly recognized it, transformed by the night and the snow. The light turned the drifts into strange sculptures that changed every time I moved. The old paths were obliterated and I wandered the new ones made by the snow. Possibly I stepped on some sleeping plants. The tatty remains of last year were covered over, a pure white blanket. A young pine was bent double. I flicked the snow off and it sprang up again, nodding.

I brushed off the bench by the magnolia and sat down. The light spread out from the house, a broad silvery gold glittering path that reached right to the magnolia. I tried to summon up Beattie to share it with her, but she was gone. It was the first time she hadn't been there. I wondered what was wrong, then remembered it was nearly a year since she'd died. I read somewhere that grief has two stages: the first terrible month, and then the first year. After that, everything goes a bit hazy. You still remember, but the memories are vague and soft. I laughed, picturing Beattie transformed into the glittering golden path that stopped at my feet. Why not?

And suddenly, a moment of pure happiness.

And after it, a curious new sensation. It was as if all the sad and ugly things that had happened moved a step away from my mind. They were still there – Camille's last trick, Mummy's treachery, Andrew's desertion, the deaths of Dominic and Daddy and Beattie, and all the years of exploitation by other people's children – but all of it was, like Beattie's ghost, somehow muted, removed from the soft centre where it could really hurt. One by one I tried them out. Memories, yes, strong and sharp like the knife-edge snowdrifts around me. But no more pain. I looked at the pure white waves of snow covering the dead autumn and wondered why spring, not winter, is the symbol of new life.

And why not a new life at forty-one? I may not be young, but I'm healthy and strong. I'm free of my mother. My job is as secure as any. Where I live doesn't matter all that much – a flat, another house. (This time I'll have the strength to close the door against children.) Perhaps Barnaby will build me a small-is-beautiful and I'll start a new garden, a haven for those few of us free from the need to own children. I'm not leaving town, either. If I belong anywhere, it's here. I've had friends here before and I'll have friends here again: Barnaby, maybe another Alice, maybe the new people who are buying my garden? There are always a few misfits in any town. I'll find them, people who'll forgive me my eccentricities and I'll forgive theirs. I know I can't change the world, and for Beattie's sake, I'm sorry. But I *can* stand to one side of it, and see, and know, and that's something.

And then I knew that the past events had not only softened but transformed themselves into something else, like Beattie transformed into the golden light coming out at me from the house. Just this: that now I understood how and why the things that had happened had happened. It may not sound much, but suddenly it mattered more than anything else.

I got up and walked back to the house along the light-path. I didn't even stop at the door and look back for a final farewell. There was no need. I wasn't losing my garden, only transferring custodianship of that which could never be owned anyway, not really. Beattie was right. All in the head, all in the mind. That much is still whole.

FOR THE BEST IN PAPERBACKS, LOOK FOR THE 🐧

In every corner of the world, on every subject under the sun, Penguin represents quality and variety – the very best in publishing today.

For complete information about books available from Penguin – including Pelicans, Puffins, Peregrines and Penguin Classics – and how to order them, write to us at the appropriate address below. Please note that for copyright reasons the selection of books varies from country to country.

In the United Kingdom: For a complete list of books available from Penguin in the U.K., please write to *Dept E.P., Penguin Books Ltd, Harmondsworth, Middlesex, UB7 0DA*

In the United States: For a complete list of books available from Penguin in the U.S., please write to *Dept BA, Penguin, 299 Murray Hill Parkway, East Rutherford, New Jersey 07073*

In Canada: For a complete list of books available from Penguin in Canada, please write to *Penguin Books Canada Ltd, 2801 John Street, Markham, Ontario L3R 1B4*

In Australia: For a complete list of books available from Penguin in Australia, please write to the *Marketing Department, Penguin Books Australia Ltd, P.O. Box 257, Ringwood, Victoria 3134*

In New Zealand: For a complete list of books available from Penguin in New Zealand, please write to the *Marketing Department, Penguin Books (NZ) Ltd, Private Bag, Takapuna, Auckland 9*

In India: For a complete list of books available from Penguin, please write to *Penguin Overseas Ltd, 706 Eros Apartments, 56 Nehru Place, New Delhi, 110019*

In Holland: For a complete list of books available from Penguin in Holland, please write to *Penguin Books Nederland B.V., Postbus 195, NL-1380AD Weesp, Netherlands*

In Germany: For a complete list of books available from Penguin, please write to *Penguin Books Ltd, Friedrichstrasse 10 – 12, D–6000 Frankfurt Main 1, Federal Republic of Germany*

In Spain: For a complete list of books available from Penguin in Spain, please write to *Longman Penguin España, Calle San Nicolas 15, E–28013 Madrid, Spain*

A CHOICE OF PENGUIN FICTION

Monsignor Quixote Graham Greene

Now filmed for television, Graham Greene's novel, like Cervantes' seventeenth-century classic, is a brilliant fable for its times. 'A deliciously funny novel' – *The Times*

The Dearest and the Best Leslie Thomas

In the spring of 1940 the spectre of war turned into grim reality – and for all the inhabitants of the historic villages of the New Forest it was the beginning of the most bizarre, funny and tragic episode of their lives. 'Excellent' – *Sunday Times*

Earthly Powers Anthony Burgess

Anthony Burgess's magnificent masterpiece, an enthralling, epic narrative spanning six decades and spotlighting some of the most vivid events and characters of our times. 'Enormous imagination and vitality . . . a huge book in every way' – Bernard Levin in the *Sunday Times*

The Penitent Isaac Bashevis Singer

From the Nobel Prize-winning author comes a powerful story of a man who has material wealth but feels spiritually impoverished. 'Singer . . . restates with dignity the spiritual aspirations and the cultural complexities of a lifetime, and it must be said that in doing so he gives the Evil One no quarter and precious little advantage' – Anita Brookner in the *Sunday Times*

Paradise Postponed John Mortimer

'Hats off to John Mortimer. He's done it again' – *Spectator*. A rumbustious, hilarious new novel from the creator of Rumpole, *Paradise Postponed* is now a major Thames Television series.

Animal Farm George Orwell

The classic political fable of the twentieth century.

A CHOICE OF PENGUIN FICTION

Maia   Richard Adams

The heroic romance of love and war in an ancient empire from one of our greatest storytellers. 'Enormous and powerful' – *Financial Times*

The Warning Bell   Lynne Reid Banks

A wonderfully involving, truthful novel about the choices a woman must make in her life – and the price she must pay for ignoring the counsel of her own heart. 'Lynne Reid Banks knows how to get to her reader: this novel grips like Super Glue' – *Observer*

Doctor Slaughter   Paul Theroux

Provocative and menacing – a brilliant dissection of lust, ambition and betrayal in 'civilized' London. 'Witty, chilly, exuberant, graphic' – *The Times Literary Supplement*

July's People   Nadine Gordimer

Set in South Africa, this novel gives us an unforgettable look at the terrifying, tacit understanding and misunderstandings between blacks and whites. 'This is the best novel that Miss Gordimer has ever written' – Alan Paton in the *Saturday Review*

Wise Virgin   A. N. Wilson

Giles Fox's work on the Pottle manuscript, a little-known thirteenth-century tract on virginity, leads him to some innovative research on the subject that takes even his breath away. 'A most elegant and chilling comedy' – *Observer* Books of the Year

Last Resorts   Clare Boylan

Harriet loved Joe Fischer for his ordinariness – for his ordinary suits and hats, his ordinary money and his ordinary mind, even for his ordinary wife. 'An unmitigated delight' – *Time Out*

A CHOICE OF PENGUIN FICTION

Stanley and the Women   Kingsley Amis

Just when Stanley Duke thinks it safe to sink into middle age, his son goes insane – and Stanley finds himself beset on all sides by women, each of whom seems to have an intimate acquaintance with madness. 'Very good, very powerful . . . beautifully written' – Anthony Burgess in the *Observer*

The Girls of Slender Means   Muriel Spark

A world and a war are winding up with a bang, and in what is left of London all the nice people are poor – and about to discover how different the new world will be. 'Britain's finest post-war novelist' – *The Times*

Him with His Foot in His Mouth   Saul Bellow

A collection of first-class short stories. 'If there is a better living writer of fiction, I'd very much like to know who he or she is' – *The Times*

Mother's Helper   Maureen Freely

A superbly biting and breathtakingly fluent attack on certain libertarian views, blending laughter, delight, rage and amazement, this is a novel you won't forget. 'A winner' – *The Times Literary Supplement*

Decline and Fall   Evelyn Waugh

A comic yet curiously touching account of an innocent plunged into the sham, brittle world of high society. Evelyn Waugh's first novel brought him immediate public acclaim and is still a classic of its kind.

Stars and Bars   William Boyd

Well-dressed, quite handsome, unfailingly polite and charming, who would guess that Henderson Dores, the innocent Englishman abroad in wicked America, has a guilty secret? 'Without doubt his best book so far . . . made me laugh out loud' – *The Times*

A CHOICE OF PENGUIN FICTION

Trade Wind   M. M. Kaye

An enthralling blend of history, adventure and romance from the author of the bestselling *The Far Pavilions*

The Ghost Writer   Philip Roth

Philip Roth's celebrated novel about a young writer who meets and falls in love with Anne Frank in New England – or so he thinks. 'Brilliant, witty and extremely elegant' – *Guardian*

Small World   David Lodge

Shortlisted for the 1984 Booker Prize, *Small World* brings back Philip Swallow and Maurice Zapp for a jet-propelled journey into hilarity. 'The most brilliant and also the funniest novel that he has written' – *London Review of Books*

Village Christmas   'Miss Read'

The village of Fairacre finds its peace disrupted by the arrival in its midst of the noisy, cheerful Emery family – and only the advent of a Christmas baby brings things back to normal. 'A sheer joy' – *Glasgow Evening Times*

Treasures of Time   Penelope Lively

Beautifully written, acutely observed, and filled with Penelope Lively's sharp but compassionate wit, *Treasures of Time* explores the relationship between the lives we live and the lives we think we live.

Absolute Beginners   Colin MacInnes

The first 'teenage' novel, the classic of youth and disenchantment, *Absolute Beginners* is part of MacInnes's famous London trilogy – and now a brilliant film. 'MacInnes caught it first – and best' – *Harpers and Queen*

FOR THE BEST IN PAPERBACKS, LOOK FOR THE 🐧

A CHOICE OF PENGUIN FICTION

Money Martin Amis

Savage, audacious and demonically witty – a story of urban excess. 'Terribly, terminally funny: laughter in the dark, if ever I heard it' – *Guardian*

Lolita Vladimir Nabokov

Shot through with Nabokov's mercurial wit, quicksilver prose and intoxicating sensuality, *Lolita* is one of the world's great love stories. 'A great book' – Dorothy Parker

Dinner at the Homesick Restaurant Anne Tyler

Through every family run memories which bind them together – in spite of everything. 'She is a witch. Witty, civilized, curious, with her radar ears and her quill pen dipped on one page in acid and on the next in orange liqueur . . . a wonderful writer' – John Leonard in *The New York Times*

Glitz Elmore Leonard

Underneath the Boardwalk, a lot of insects creep. But the creepiest of all was Teddy. 'After finishing *Glitz*, I went out to the bookstore and bought everything else of Elmore Leonard I could find' – Stephen King

The Battle of Pollocks Crossing J. L. Carr

Nominated for the Booker McConnell Prize, this is a moving, comic masterpiece. 'Wayward, ambiguous, eccentric . . . a fascinatingly outlandish novel' – *Guardian*

The Dreams of an Average Man Dyan Sheldon

Tony Rivera is lost. Sandy Grossman Rivera is leaving. And Maggie Kelly is giving up. In the steamy streets of summertime Manhattan, the refugees of the sixties generation wonder what went wrong. 'Satire, dramatic irony and feminist fun . . . lively, forceful and funny' – *Listener*

A CHOICE OF PENGUIN FICTION

Bliss Jill Tweedie

When beautiful Lady Clare La Fontaine marries for money, she enters a glittering world of luxury and corruption and discovers the darker side of sexual politics in Jill Tweedie's blockbusting, bestselling novel. 'Huge, vital and passionately written' – *Cosmopolitan*

Fair Stood the Wind for France H. E. Bates

It was France, and wartime – and not the moment to fall in love. 'Perhaps the finest novel of the war . . . a lovely book which makes the heart beat with pride' – *Daily Telegraph*

The Flight from the Enchanter Iris Murdoch

A group of people have elected ambiguous and fascinating Mischa Fox to be their god. And thus begins the battle between sturdy common sense and dangerous enchantment. Elegant, sparkling and unputdownable, this is Iris Murdoch at her best.

Very Good, Jeeves! P. G. Wodehouse

When Bertie Wooster lands in the soup, only the 'infinite sagacity' of Jeeves can pull him out. 'A riot . . . There are eleven tales in this volume and each is the best' – *Observer*

To Have and To Hold Deborah Moggach

Viv was giving her sister, Ann, the best present she could think of – a baby. How Viv, Ann and their husbands cope with this extraordinary situation is the subject of this tender, triumphant and utterly absorbing story. Now a powerful TV drama.

A Dark and Distant Shore Reay Tannahill

Vilia is the unforgettable heroine, Kinveil Castle is her destiny, in this full-blooded saga spanning a century of Victoriana, empire, hatred and love affairs. 'A marvellous blend of *Gone with the Wind* and *The Thorn Birds*' – *Daily Mirror*

A CHOICE OF PENGUIN FICTION

Other Women Lisa Alther

From the bestselling author of *Kinflicks* comes this compelling novel of today's woman – and a heroine with whom millions of women will identify.

Your Lover Just Called John Updike

Stories of Joan and Richard Maple – a couple multiplied by love and divided by lovers. Here is the portrait of a modern American marriage in all its mundane moments and highs and lows of love as only John Updike could draw it.

Mr Love and Justice Colin MacInnes

Frankie Love took up his career as a ponce about the same time as Edward Justice became vice-squad detective. Except that neither man was particularly suited for his job, all they had in common was an interest in crime. But, as any ponce or copper will tell you, appearances are not always what they seem. Provocative and honest and acidly funny, *Mr Love and Justice* is the final volume of Colin MacInnes's famous London trilogy.

An Ice-Cream War William Boyd

As millions are slaughtered on the Western Front, a ridiculous and little-reported campaign is being waged in East Africa – a war they continued after the Armistice because no one told them to stop. 'A towering achievement' – John Carey, Chairman of the Judges of the 1982 Booker Prize, for which this novel was nominated.

Every Day is Mother's Day Hilary Mantel

An outrageous story of lust, adultery, madness, death and the social services. 'Strange . . . rather mad . . . extremely funny . . . she sometimes reminded me of the early Muriel Spark' – Auberon Waugh

1982 Janine Alasdair Gray

Set inside the head of an ageing, divorced, alcoholic, insomniac supervisor of security installations who is tippling in the bedroom of a small Scottish hotel – this is a most brilliant and controversial novel.